THE
GUILTY
MAN

An absolutely gripping crime mystery with a massive twist

HELEN H. DURRANT

Detectives Lennox & Wilde Thrillers Book 1

D0012112

JOFFE
BOOKS

First published in Great Britain 2020
Joffe Books, London
www.joffebooks.com

Please join our mailing list for free Kindle books and new releases.

www.joffebooks.com

We love to hear from our readers! Please email any feedback you have to: feedback@joffebooks.com

ISBN 978-1-78931-581-3

For my lovely granddaughter, Layla,
on her eighteenth birthday x

PROLOGUE

A piercing scream echoed against the bare walls, inhuman, a noise to ice the blood. The victim was weeping. In the space of a few hours this villain, who was more used to meting out torment than receiving it, had been reduced to an abject, quivering bundle. He was pleading for his life.

The man smiled to himself. He was good at this.

He moved closer to inspect the damage he'd inflicted and shook his head. A shoddy job. Blood was pouring from the stump where the victim's left hand used to be. The amputation had been rushed and for several hours his victim had been unconscious. He'd had a go at cauterising the wound to stop the bleeding, but it hadn't gone well.

"That must hurt," he said with some interest. The man dangling above him whimpered. "Do you realise it's gone, Nick? I'm curious to know if what they say is true and it feels like it's still there."

Not daring to look down at what had been done to him, the victim shook his head, swaying slightly on the rope. "Let . . . let me go. I'll pay you."

Tempting. Nick was worth a fortune. Accept and he'd be wealthy, free to wave his old life goodbye for good. But Nick had a fearful reputation round here. His was the name

1

you whispered and hoped no one overheard. No, Nick would never let it lie. Despite his own reputation and good connections, no way could he accept the offer.

"Nice one, Nick, but I'll have to decline. Anyway, it's getting late, time to call it a day. I've still got a lot of preparation to do, and it'll take a while. I must say I'm not looking forward to the next bit, all the clearing up. You see, the people I'm working for don't want anything left behind for the police." He smiled at the terrified man. "Sorry it had to end like this, Nick, but I have no choice."

"No . . . no, you can't. I'll give you anything — money, property, a share in the business."

"Desperate, eh? It sounds all wrong coming from your mouth. Just look at what you've been reduced to. What a way to end up."

"Who . . . who set this up?" Nick gasped. "At least tell me that before you kill me."

He smiled. "Guess. Go on, see if you can come up with the right name. In fact, I'll do you a deal. Guess right and I'll let you go free."

He'd no intention of doing anything of the sort. But he'd enjoy seeing the disappointment on Nick's face when he said the obvious and learned it was someone else entirely.

CHAPTER ONE

"Harry! Wake up. C'mon, move it, we've got a shout," Detective Sergeant Jess Wilde said. "Move your lazy arse for God's sake. We've got to go."

"Bugger off, Jess. It's my day off."

"Not anymore, sunshine, this is urgent."

DI Harry Lennox's blond, dishevelled head surfaced from under the bedding. He squinted at the daylight and groaned. "Leave me be. I'm not well."

"Hungover, you mean. You had a skinful last night. You look dreadful and this place stinks," she said.

"I'm doing just fine." Who was he kidding? He was just about getting by.

"You're living in a beat-up camper van on a mate's drive for God's sake. You've got little in the way of facilities and you're drunk most nights. Carry on like this and you'll not only have no home, you'll be out of a job too!"

Much as he liked Jess and valued her opinions, Harry didn't need this. He was too tired. He knew his life was a mess, and he could do without her shoving the fact down his throat. He had a splitting headache and was in desperate need of sleep. He'd been up half the night playing poker with Don, the man whose drive he was living on. Not that he was particularly fond of poker, but that and the booze served as a distraction from the dark stuff in his head.

Jess punched him, making him wince. Why the sudden lack of sympathy? She was usually all right, knew the chaos his life was in and said she understood. So, what was up with her today? "Okay, okay, I give in. What's so urgent that you've dragged yourself over here at this unearthly hour?"

"Lucy Green has turned up."

Jess Wilde couldn't have sobered him up quicker if she'd thrown a bucket of water over him. Harry Lennox felt as if he'd been kicked in the guts. He'd been dreading this day, having to face her mother with the news, and seeing the whole dreadful business plastered all over the press yet again.

His voice shaking, he said, "How d'you know it's her? It's been five weeks. Is the body still recognisable?"

"Very much so. She was found wandering around Cheetham Park an hour ago by a member of the public . The woman was concerned because Lucy had nothing on her feet and was dressed only in a cotton frock."

Harry Lennox didn't understand. Three-year-old Lucy Green had disappeared without a trace. They'd subsequently found evidence indicating that she'd been murdered. The investigation had been extensive, costing a fortune, eventually leading the team to a man called Albert Sykes. He'd been arrested, had confessed to killing her and was awaiting trial. He had been interviewed countless times but always refused to say what he'd done with the body.

The evidence against Sykes was compelling — one of Lucy's toys, a pink teddy bear she was fond of, was found in his possession as well as traces of her blood on his shirt. He'd made a weak excuse about her falling over and grazing her knee, but given his reputation no one believed it for a second. CCTV footage showed him talking to the little girl in the park where she'd disappeared. He was then clearly seen taking her hand and leading her away. That was the last time Lucy Green had been seen alive. Until today.

"Has she said anything, like what happened or where she's been?"

"You don't know much about kids, do you?" Jess scoffed. "Lucy is only three, she's little more than an infant. The doctor reckons she's been given something. Right now, she doesn't even know her name."

Lennox threw back the duvet and gingerly got to his feet. His body ached all over and he felt sick. He made yet another resolution to knock the strong ale on the head.

Jess chucked a dressing gown at him. "Cover yourself up and don't insult my eyes. I don't want to see any more of you than I have to if it's all the same to you."

He gave her a cheeky grin. Who was she kidding? Jess liked him really, she just wouldn't admit it. She wasn't bad-looking either. Strawberry blonde hair, neat figure and with just the right amount of attitude. "I'll go inside the house and get a shower. You can make us some coffee."

"We don't have time for coffee. Clean yourself up, put on some decent clothes and we'll be off. Lucy is with social services until they find her mother. We need to speak to the child before that witch poisons her head. We also need to speak to the woman who found her, and anyone else who was in that area of the park this morning."

"Busy day ahead then."

Lennox wrapped himself in the dressing gown and disappeared. The kid was alive and that was brilliant. But where the hell had she been? He really didn't want to think about what Lucy Green might have suffered in the time she was missing. Albert Sykes had only been in custody for the last three weeks. Prior to that, he would have been able to do what he liked with the girl.

Albert had worn the label 'perv' around his neck for most of his life. He'd been in that park at the same time as Lucy, had been seen holding her hand, and no one had got so much as a glimpse of her after that. Combined with the other evidence, the blood and particularly finding her teddy in that damn shopping bag he always carried around with him, his fate had been sealed.

No bail meant Albert had to await trial inside. The other inmates had soon learned what he'd been accused of and made his life a misery. Their bullying culminated in a brutal attack which put Albert in hospital. Currently, he was hooked up to a ventilator in Ryebridge General.

The hot water slaked over him, bringing some relief to his aching body, but the thoughts in his head weren't so easily washed away. What if Albert Sykes was innocent? The man was badly injured, he could die. What then? Would it be their fault?

Ten minutes later he was ready to go, showered, hair brushed and sporting a clean shirt and a suit.

Jess smiled when he walked in. "If I didn't know what you're really like, I might think you're a bit of a stunner. When you ditch the slob, you remind me of one of those moody early sixties pop stars. Turn up your jacket collar, strike a pose and you could have a new career."

"Not something I aspire to." He smiled. "Suit's not mine either, I'm afraid. It's Don's. There's a pile of washing in that basket when I get time to go to the laundrette. But most of my stuff is still at the house — that is if Anthea hasn't thrown it all away."

"Really hates you then, does she?"

"Afraid so. I just wish I knew what I've done wrong."

Jess rolled her eyes.

CHAPTER TWO

They had arranged to meet Lucy and her mum at the kiddies' playroom in the offices of the social services on Stamford Road. When Harry and Jess arrived, Lucy was playing happily with a young woman social worker. Kelsey, her mother, was pacing the floor, arms folded and a sour expression on her face.

"Look at her," Jess whispered. "She should be over the moon. Instead, I swear the witch is disappointed."

"What the 'ell d'you two want?" Kelsey asked, spitting her gum into a bin. "The kid's okay, anyone can see that. Night in her own bed and she'll be back to normal."

"We'd like to speak to her," Harry said.

He gave the woman his best boyish smile, which wasn't lost on Jess. Lennox could be quite the charmer when he chose.

"We won't bother her for long," he said. "We just want to see if she recalls anything at all."

"She doesn't," Kelsey snapped. "The doctor's examined her and she's fine. And Lucy hasn't been . . . you know, tampered with."

Harry nodded, relieved. That was something at least. But they still needed to find out where the child had been. "Has she said anything?"

"Not much. Mind you, she never does. The clinic reckon she's a bit behind, not reaching her milestones or whatever. Load of rubbish if you ask me. Kid's healthy enough, eats and sleeps all right. What more do they expect?"

Something occurred to Jess. "Kelsey, does Lucy talk at all?"

The woman gave Jess a filthy look. "Hardly. She gabbles on, to her toys and the like. I've no idea what about, can't make out half of it."

Jess looked at Harry and shook her head. Kelsey Green was a disgrace.

A woman who'd been sitting in the corner taking notes came forward. "Rhoda Jackson, social services. The Green family has been one of mine since Lucy was born. I'm compiling a report on what we've got so far regarding this incident, not that it's much. However, I can confirm that according to the doctor who examined her, Lucy does not appear to have been harmed in any way." She ushered the detectives out of the mother's earshot. "In fact, the child is in better condition than when she disappeared. She's been well fed, even put on weight, and the clothes she was found in were an expensive, designer brand."

"A cotton frock?" Jess said.

"Yes, one of those with fancy smocking on the chest and embroidered on the pockets, plus matching underwear," Rhoda confirmed.

"But there was nothing on her feet — a bit of a contradiction that," Jess said.

"The police are searching the area," Rhoda Jackson said. "They may yet find the footwear. Kelsey told me earlier that Lucy is a devil for discarding her shoes and running around barefoot."

"Is the child up to talking to us?" Harry Lennox asked.

"No, she's still quite sleepy. The doctor suspects she was given a mild sedative before she was found."

"Has she said anything?"

"She's asked for Clara, if that helps."

It didn't, not unless the mother could shed some light. Jess turned to look at her.

Rhoda Jackson looked unimpressed. "Oh, I've asked her, and no, Ms Green has no idea. Nor does she appear particularly interested in what has happened to her daughter or where she's been. If I'm honest, I have serious doubts about allowing the woman to take Lucy home. All she seems to be interested in is how much the press will pay her for the story."

Harry frowned. Kelsey must not talk about this to anyone, not yet. There was still evidence to collect and collate. Until they had a better picture of what had happened, all the press would be told was that the child was back and unharmed.

"Kelsey!" he called to her. "A word."

She approached, hands on hips. "How long do we have to stay here? I've got stuff to do."

"That's up to Ms Jackson. In the meantime, you must not talk to the press. Do you understand?"

"Why not, copper? She's my kid. It'll bring in some welcome cash. I can't afford not to sell her story to the highest bidder."

"You must wait until we give you the okay," Harry insisted. "Otherwise you could jeopardise our investigations."

"No need to bother investigating anything now, is there? It's all over. She's back and okay. I'm fine with that. I don't stir the pot, that's what I say."

"Not the way it works, I'm afraid," Harry said.

Kelsey shrugged and walked off, calling over her shoulder to the woman playing with Lucy, "I'm off outside for a fag."

"I'll go round to the home, do an assessment and make sure Lucy is safe and being cared for properly," Rhoda said.

"She isn't though, is she?" Jess replied. "How come the poor kid went missing in the first place? How did that happen?"

"That is still under review. The statements off Kelsey and other witnesses at the time told us Lucy had gone to the park with a friend of Kelsey's that day. Everyone there was spoken to, and all of them confirmed that when Lucy disappeared, that woman was several metres away, chatting with a group of blokes. They in turn were questioned but remembered nothing."

"So, a couple of three-year-olds were left to their own devices?" Jess asked.

Rhoda nodded. "Which is why there'll be a full assessment."

"Will Kelsey be allowed to take Lucy home today?" Jess asked.

"That's a delicate matter. We've broached it with her, but she's sworn to make trouble if we don't allow it. You know, tell the press, get them on her side. We can't afford a witch hunt against the department. All we want is for the child to be safe. Initially, we will go down the close-monitoring route. Don't worry, we know the score and our people are on the ball."

"We'll need to know what's happening with the child," Harry said. "We'd still like to try and talk to her at some point."

"What will you do about the man in prison, the one who took her?" Rhoda asked.

"*Allegedly* took her. He's in hospital," Jess said. "He was seen in the park that day, and he's admitted to taking and subsequently killing Lucy, which is obviously a lie. We'll speak to him again and hope he tells the truth this time."

CHAPTER THREE

"Can we get something to eat before we check in at the station?" Harry asked.

"I thought you felt sick."

"That was then, Jess. Now I'm starving."

"Café in the shopping mall? Fancy going there?"

"Good choice. They do a neat bacon butty."

"Where's the kid been these last weeks, then?" Jess asked.

"Given how well she looked, I'd say nowhere near her mother."

"I don't like Kelsey Green much either, Harry, but she's still the kid's mother and her sole guardian."

"No father?"

"He's dead. He and Kelsey never married but he did live with them for a while. Roddy Barrett, remember him? Got on the wrong side of a dealer and ended up in the canal," Jess said.

"Poor kid," Harry said. "How we continue with the case will be down to Rodders now. He might even put the other team on it."

'Rodders' was Superintendent Roderick Croft, who led the two teams at the station.

"You know what he's like. He'll say we've had our chance," Jess said. "After all, Sykes did confess, so he'll be keen to pass it on. Which isn't fair. In any case, I'd like to re-interview the other people who were in the park that afternoon."

"But first we'll speak to the folk who were there today, and the woman who spotted Lucy," Harry added.

Ryebridge shopping mall was practically empty. High rents and unemployment in the area had led to at least half of the shops closing down. It was market day too, so folk preferred to wander around there, and the detectives had the café to themselves.

They were regular customers and Elsie Pike, the owner, had come to like them. She looked Harry up and down and gave him an approving smile. "You look sharp this morning — interview or something?"

"No, Elsie, just trying a different look," he said.

"You should make the effort more often. Nice clothes make you look as if you know what you're doing." She laughed. "I'll bring the food over. Usual, is it?"

"That one's got the measure of you, Lennox," Jess said. "And you'd better watch the suit. Don won't want it back covered in brown sauce."

He nodded and then pulled a face. "He's a good mate for letting me borrow what I need, but I'll have to get my own stuff back off Anthea. I'll nip round to the house later, see if she's in a better mood."

Jess shook her head. "Good luck with that one."

Harry and his partner had split a month ago. Anthea had a vicious temper and seemed determined not to give an inch. But despite what Jess thought of the woman, she felt she had to suggest a compromise. "Have you considered making things right with her, giving your relationship another go? At least then you'd have somewhere to live."

"We can't go back to how we were, and anyway, I was getting tired of living at her place. She made me feel like a kept man. Something had to change, Anthea made that crystal. She told me in no uncertain terms that I couldn't keep the job and her. So, what was I supposed to do? The job's my life, my independence. I can't just jack it in, not for her or anyone. Anthea reckons another woman would have been easier to deal with."

"Anthea knew what she was taking on. Why the ultimatum now?"

"The night-time call outs were what finally did it, and we've had a lot recently. Can't do without her beauty sleep, you see."

Anthea was a selfish bitch. All she cared about was herself. She'd no idea what she was putting Harry through. Making him choose between her and the job was just cruel. Underneath the untidiness and his chaotic lifestyle, Harry was okay, and he was easy on the eye. Any girl would give her eye teeth for those chiselled cheekbones and blonde hair.

They'd worked together since his transfer from West Yorkshire two years ago and got along well. Apart from the way he was currently living, the only other thing that irritated her about Harry was his reluctance to talk about himself. Jess couldn't understand why. He'd worked in Bradford, but he had a Scottish accent, so that was obviously where he came from, but he refused to say anything about his background.

"You can't live on Don's drive for much longer," she told him. "You've no washing or cooking facilities. If you and Anthea are really over, you have to get yourself a place of your own."

"Says the thirty-year-old who still lives with her mum and dad."

Jess cuffed him lightly across the head. "That's how it is these days. I'm saving for a house. It won't be long now."

"You serious?" he asked.

"Absolutely. My parents are helping me with the deposit, I've got savings, I've spoken to the bank and got a mortgage in principle. Basically, I'm all set to go."

"So, what's stopping you?"

"Finding the courage to make the leap," she admitted. "I've looked at those new-builds at the back of Cheetham Park in the 'bridge. They're within my price range and quite spacious for new houses."

Lennox was impressed. "Been inside one yet?"

"Last weekend. The one I'd go for has a view over the park and towards the hills. There's a small garden front and back and a garage."

"I'm well jealous now,' he said. 'No way I'll be able to save enough for a deposit. Looks like I'm going to have to rent for the foreseeable."

"Try harder," she said. "Give up the booze for starters, that'll save you a packet. Problem sorted."

"I don't have the temperament for saving."

"You can't continue the way you are. What about your parents, Harry? Mine are helping me, aren't yours able to help? At least, loan you some money?"

It was a casual enough question, but it seemed to upset him. His face fell. "I'm on my own, I'm afraid."

"I'm sure if you explain the circumstances," Jess persisted, "they'd do their best." He looked away. Talking about his parents was making him squirm. Why was that? Why was he so reluctant to discuss any aspect of his family life? "You've never said much about your family, where you come from or any of it. We've been together long enough, you know plenty about me. One could be forgiven for thinking you were hiding some dark secret." She smiled.

"You've found me out." He grinned briefly, then his face fell again. "I haven't had a happy past, Jess." He held up his heavily scarred hands. "These injuries on my fingers are the result of burns. I'm incredibly lucky to still have the use of them. The incident that caused them belongs to my past, and I don't like to drag it up. All I want is to forget, start again. So, drop it, Jess. Please."

This was always how it was whenever she brought up his history. Harry Lennox was determined to remain a mystery, and Jess had a feeling that it wasn't just about what had happened to his hands.

"When are you taking the plunge and moving out then?" he asked, changing the subject.

Jess shook her head. "It's not that easy. Getting the mortgage is one thing, but will I be able to afford the bills? I've been doing my sums and it's quite an amount. At the mo, I bung my mum some housekeeping each month and that's that. Go it alone and I'll be responsible for the lot."

"You know what you need, Jessie, don't you? A lodger."

CHAPTER FOUR

The police station was housed in a large Victorian red-brick building on Ryebridge's main road. Impressive from the outside, in reality the high ceilings and the antiquated heating meant the rooms were like ice in winter, and very draughty. The roof leaked and there wasn't a window in the place that didn't rattle in the wind. But on the plus side, it wasn't far from where either of them lived, and was handy for the shops.

One day they might build a new one, but Harry wouldn't hold his breath. Ryebridge was a small northern town with little in the way of industry and an economy rapidly going downhill. Completely unremarkable, it was simply a dot on the map, to the right of the M1 going south. Its one redeeming feature was its position in the crook of the Pennines, which could be seen from most properties in the town. Ryebridge was a perfect place to run to, the perfect place to hide. Which is why Harry had chosen it.

As he and Jess entered the main CID office, they were met by Superintendent Croft. "Good of you both to show," he snapped. "I tried your mobile, Lennox, no answer. Do us both a favour and turn the bloody thing on, would you?"

Only then did Harry realise that in the rush to see Lucy he'd left it in the camper van. "Sorry, sir. What's so urgent?"

"We've got Caroline Sutton in the soft interview room. Her husband Nick has disappeared."

Not about Lucy Green then. Harry caught his breath. Nick Sutton was what passed for a big-time villain round here. They'd never been able to pin anything on him, but he was behind at least half of the crime, including most of the drug dealing, that went on in their area. The rest was down to his arch-rival, Andy Marsh. His disappearance, if true, should be celebrated, not investigated. Ryebridge might be unremarkable but it still had all the problems of the modern world, and its poverty exacerbated them.

"Caroline Sutton? And you want me to speak to her?" Harry was puzzled by his super's request. "Is that a good idea, sir, given our last encounter? Had I convinced her to come clean about that man who was beaten black and blue, we might have Sutton locked up for now. As it was, she accused me of bullying and made an official complaint."

Harry was thinking of a case he'd handled a few months ago. He'd been within a spit of getting Sutton under lock and key, but his wife had refused to speak out against him. Instead, she gave him the alibi that kept him out of prison.

"Which wasn't upheld," Croft said. "Anyway, all that is irrelevant now. For some reason, Caroline Sutton has asked for you by name. Tread carefully, keep it polite and report back to me when you've finished, got that?"

Harry Lennox nodded. He had no choice.

"Be very careful, Harry," Jess warned him as soon as Croft had gone. "That woman is as sly as they come. She's asked for you for a reason, don't get sucked in."

"Odd though, don't you think? Nick Sutton's wife walks into a police station and asks for help. You couldn't make it up."

Caroline Sutton was seated on a sofa sipping coffee. She was an attractive woman of about forty, with dark hair cut in a bob. Her clothes were immaculate and top of the range. Harry had seen those shoes in a boutique in Manchester when he'd been on a shopping trip with Anthea. She'd pointed them out, and the price had made his eyes water. Caroline looked up and smiled when he entered the room. She patted the seat next to her.

"I owe you an apology, DI Lennox," she said. "I shouldn't have sounded off like that the last time we met. Very ill-mannered of me."

"I've got broad shoulders," he said, choosing to sit on a seat opposite her. "I believe Nick's gone missing?"

"Yes, and I'm really worried. It's not like him to just disappear without saying anything. We've not had words, and he had no plans. I have a bad feeling about this." She took another sip of her coffee and frowned. "I'm not going to pretend. We both know what Nick is, and because of that, he has enemies. Recently he's had a couple of serious run-ins with Andy Marsh."

Harry knew what that meant — a possible new turf war. Sutton and Marsh had maintained an uneasy truce for months now, but it was never expected to last. The pair were bitter rivals after all.

"So, you think Nick's disappearance is down to Marsh?" he asked.

"They've been at it again lately, sniping over the phone, threatening each other. Nick was genuinely worried this time. Marsh told him he was making a play for the Baxendale and Nick knew that would mean carnage. The opposing gangs would fight, and heaven help anyone who got in the way."

The Baxendale was a sink estate on the edge of Ryebridge. Built in the fifties as an overspill for the Manchester terraces that were being cleared, it had had a bad reputation from the start, which only deteriorated down the years. Today all the houses on the estate — hundreds of them — were rundown, as were the four blocks of flats. Most of the tenants didn't work, surviving on their wits or dealing drugs. A lot of them worked for either Sutton or Marsh, running errands in the parts of the estate they controlled.

"Did Nick do anything about Marsh's threats?" Harry asked.

"I had a word with him, told him it wasn't worth it. We don't need the hassle. I don't know if Nick took what I said seriously but the last time they spoke was the day before he disappeared, and they were still at each other's throats."

"Is any of his stuff missing — clothes and the like?"

"No, his wardrobe was the first thing I checked. I've tried his mobile and it's dead."

"How long has he been gone?" Harry asked.

"Since yesterday morning. He should have been back by five, but there's been no word and no sign."

"Sorry to ask this, Mrs Sutton, but could Nick have gone off with another woman, do you think?"

Her expression froze. "Our marriage is solid. Nick has never strayed, and he never would. He's a lot of things, Harry, but he's not unfaithful."

"And you've really no idea where he might be?"

"Do you imagine I'd walk in here, ask to speak to you, if I had a choice? You've had dealings with Nick, you know him. He's missing, and I'm terrified that something dreadful has happened to him. In ten years of marriage, not once has he left me overnight without telling me exactly where he was going and when he'd be back."

"The problem we have is that Nick is an adult, and as such, he's free to come and go as he chooses. In cases like this we don't usually class a person as even missing until they've been gone forty-eight hours. Unless we have evidence that he's come to harm or is in danger, there's not a lot we can do until that time has passed. Do you have any evidence that he's in danger?"

Harry half expected the woman to launch a torrent of abuse at him and flounce out, but that's not what happened. Instead, she shook her head. Tears welled up in her eyes and began to trickle down her cheeks. Caroline meant every word. She was genuinely worried. Harry finally accepted that Nick Sutton was missing.

CHAPTER FIVE

It was dark and there wasn't much lighting on the Baxendale. Advantageous for some, but Kelsey Green was scared. She wouldn't normally risk going out at night, not round here, but she had no choice. She had to find someone, some young bloke who could help her. Give her what she needed.

She spotted a hooded figure pass by. "Hey!" she hissed, "Over here."

"What's up, Kel? Be sharp, I've got stuff to do."

He knew her but she'd no idea who he was, just a face who sold drugs for one of the dealers. "Have you got summat — you know, calm my nerves? It's been a rough few days."

"Got money?"

"No, but I'll be getting some soon. The papers'll give me a fortune for my story when I'm allowed to speak out. I'll pay you then," she said.

The lad shook his head. "Sorry, Kel. No can do. I have orders off the boss — no money, no gear. Come back when you can pay."

Kelsey watched the lad shuffle off into the darkness. She swore. She needed a fix or she'd go mad. What right had that stupid copper to order her to keep quiet? Lucy was her kid and it was their story. Kelsey would tell who she liked.

20

She heard someone call to her from the gloom. "Kel!" She looked around but could see nothing. "Kel. Over here."

Kelsey made out a giant of a man standing in one of the passageways that ran between the rows of houses. She'd seen him around but didn't know his name, neither did she know which dealer he worked for. Smiling nervously, she walked towards him. "Hi. I need something. Can you help me?"

He fished in his pocket and took out a handful of small packets. "As much as you want. Here, have them all. Pay me when you can."

Kelsey Green couldn't believe her luck. "You sure? You won't get into trouble?"

"After new customers, aren't we? Got a different boss now. Instructions are to get new trade. Fill your boots and tell your friends."

She didn't need telling twice. Kelsey stuffed the bags into her pockets before he had a chance to change his mind. "I won't forget this. You've saved my life."

* * *

Harry yawned. "Time to make tracks. Think I'll get a takeaway on my way home and have an early night."

Jess shuddered. "I don't know how you sleep in that camper thing. God knows what's lurking in the cupboards or crawling about in the seating. You have to find somewhere else. Why don't you go and speak to Anthea, see if she's feeling a bit friendlier?"

Harry was about to answer when the door opened and an excited-looking uniformed officer burst in. "We've found the kid's shoes, sir! We were searching along the path that leads from the playground back to the road, and her shoes were there. They looked as if she'd just stepped out of them. We've had them sent over to forensics."

"Make sure that path is taped off and get someone to watch it tonight. We don't want the locals trampling all over any evidence," Harry said. "We'll have a look tomorrow in daylight, but I doubt we'll find much. What's the betting Lucy was dropped off in a car and told to go into the park on foot?"

"The CSI bods will take a look tomorrow. If there is any evidence of who dropped her there, they'll find it. There's a pull-in nearby, might be tyre tracks on that, and we'll check all the CCTV," the officer said.

"I'll sort someone to watch it before I go," Harry said.

"Right then. I'll leave you to it." The PC hurried out.

Harry rang the Reid Centre. This was the facility that carried out the post-mortems and did the forensic investigations for the teams at the station.

Dr Hettie Trent, one of the forensic scientists at the centre, took his call. She sounded pleased to hear his voice. "Yes, Harry, we've got the shoes and they're next on the list. But I can tell you this straight off — like the dress she was wearing, they're high-end and, given how fast kids grow, she'd most likely been fitted for them."

That was something. "Will you check if there's anything on them, the soles for instance, that might tell us where Lucy has been?"

"We know the drill, Harry, we've done this sort of stuff before, you know. Don't worry, I'll get the results to you as quick as I can."

Hettie was okay, pleasant on the eye and, like Harry, in her mid-thirties. He had taken her out a couple of times since he split with Anthea, but she was another one — the camper van put her off. He'd taken her back there for a drink one time, but she wouldn't even sit down. Jess was right. If he was to have any sort of love life, he would have to sort something and fast.

He stopped and spoke to a young uniformed PC in the office. "You've got kids. Where d'you go to buy their shoes, have their feet measured and that?"

"We go to Allen's on Ryebridge Road. I think everyone does. They're expensive, but you can't skimp on kiddie's footwear — growing feet and all that."

"Do they have CCTV, d'you reckon?" Harry asked.

"They might."

"Find out, will you, and if they do or there are cameras in the vicinity, get copies of the footage, say for the last couple of days to be sure. Have a good look through and see if you can spot Lucy Green."

Harry saw the look on the PC's face. Nobody liked going through CCTV footage, it was a horrendous task. There'd be hours of the stuff. But someone had to do it and who knew, it might turn up something useful.

CHAPTER SIX

Day Two

Despite his good intentions, it had been another late one for Harry. Don, his mate, a crate of that strong brown ale he was so fond of and hours spent playing cards. The following morning Harry was dragged from a deep sleep by the sound of his mobile ringing. It was Croft, and he didn't sound happy.

"Get out of your pit and round to the Sutton household pronto. Someone's left the lovely Caroline a nasty surprise on her doorstep."

Just what he needed after all that ale. "Er, how nasty, sir?"

"Very, Lennox. A severed hand. The woman is in shock and worried out of her wits about what might have happened to her husband."

Harry's stomach sank. "We can't be sure it's him though, can we, sir? Not until the Reid run tests. I take it that's where the, er, body part has gone?"

"Well, we could hardly leave it in situ, could we? Far too horrific, and Caroline Sutton was becoming hysterical. As for being sure it's him, his wedding ring was still on his finger. It's distinctive and a tight fit. Of course, the Reid will run tests, his prints are on file so we should know pretty soon.

I want you to talk to Caroline. Find out all you can about Nick's recent dealings. If that hand really is his, then he's upset someone big time."

"When we chatted yesterday, Caroline told me that Nick had been arguing with Andy Marsh recently. She said Marsh was making a play for the Baxendale," Harry said.

"That could be our answer, but we won't jump to conclusions. Interview the woman, see what else she can tell you. Follow up on everything including Marsh. But be careful."

As Croft finished the call there was a loud bang on the door. Seconds later, Jess let herself in.

He grinned at her. "You've caught me out again. Give me five and I'll be with you."

"You don't get any better, Lennox," she said. "You need to buck your ideas up. Croft's not daft. He cottons on to your current lifestyle and he won't be happy."

"Stuff Croft. Give me five and we'll get round to the Sutton house."

"But I thought we were looking into the Lucy Green kidnap today."

"And we will, once we've visited Caroline Sutton." Jess looked disappointed. She was keen to find out what had happened to the little girl, he knew. "I have no choice, orders from Croft. Get to the bottom of what's going on with Nick and I'll be the golden boy again."

"Big-headed sod!"

"You love me really. Go on, admit it, I'm the most exciting thing in your life."

Jess laughed. "If that were true, I'd give up. And I have plenty of excitement, thank you very much."

"No man though. Strange that, 'cause you're not bad-looking in a geeky sort of way."

Jess picked up a cushion and threw it at him. "Geeky indeed! Go and get cleaned up. I'll wait in the car. There's no way I am sitting down in here."

* * *

The Suttons' home on the outskirts of Ryebridge was a large modern detached, surrounded by woodland. "Live in some style the Suttons, don't they?" Jess said. "Crime must pay after all."

"Nick Sutton does have a legitimate business too, a string of car sales showrooms he runs with his brother, Craig. Perhaps the money came from them."

Jess gave him a look. "If you believe that, you're more gullible than I thought. Sutton runs the Baxendale — drugs, loans, girls, the lot. That's where the money comes from."

"There has to be something else too, something legitimate to clean up all those earnings," Harry said.

"Well, then there's the car sales business you just mentioned," Jess said.

"Wonder what that makes?" he mused. "I'm also wondering how extensive the dealing really is. The Baxendale is a poverty-stricken hole, Sutton has to be selling elsewhere too."

"Poverty stricken or not, people can always find money for drugs and booze," Jess said. "I mean, look at you. Anyway, how do we play this?"

"Gently. The woman is distraught. Caroline and Nick Sutton have been together since they were in their teens. I've never heard any rumours about either of them straying, so I think it's safe to say they really love each other."

"You like her, don't you?" Jess said. "She won you over the other day. It's what she does. Remember that incident with her dog a few months ago, the one that went missing? Well, she praised the PC who found the mutt to high heaven. She wanted to reward him when he took it back, but when he refused, she settled for leaving that expensive box of biscuits in the main office instead. That's why Croft is soft on her."

"I wondered where they had come from."

"Go easy, Harry. I don't want you getting sucked in. That woman is — or was — married to the most dangerous man in Ryebridge, so watch your step."

They parked on the driveway under the shade of a large oak tree in full leaf. Jess noticed Caroline watching them from an upstairs window.

Jess was worried. Caroline was an attractive woman and Harry was a sucker for a pretty face. He'd have to watch his step. "C'mon, let's get on with it."

Joan Pickford, Caroline's PA, showed them into a sitting room and offered coffee. "I'll tell her you're here. Please understand that this has come as a terrible shock. So bad, in fact, that I doubt Caroline will ever recover. Nick was her life. They've been together since their early teens."

While Joan Pickford left them to go and get Caroline, Jess took the opportunity to look at the photos scattered about the room. "Small family — just the parents, Nick and his brother and that's about it," she said. "They never had any children. I wonder why if they are so close."

"None of ours, Jess, and don't ask, not today."

Caroline flung open the door. "Have you found him? Is he okay?"

"Sorry, no, not yet," Harry said.

"Do you know who . . . who could have done that to my Nick? You have no idea how dreadful it was, seeing that . . . that *thing* on the doorstep. I tried to get some sleep, but I can't stop thinking about what he must have gone through, how he's suffered. It haunts me." She sat down and burst into tears.

"Perhaps we should come back when you've recovered a bit from the shock," Harry said.

Caroline's head jerked up and she stared at them, her eyes hard. "I'll talk to you now. No point waiting. You see, I'll never get over this. Nick was my husband, my life. I don't know if I can go on living without him."

"Okay, but understand that we need you to be honest with us, Caroline. And I mean honest." Harry looked at her intently. "If that hand does belong to Nick, we need you to tell us everything about his business dealings, legal and otherwise. You must tell us about everyone who came to the house, everyone that rang him, who he mixed with."

Caroline nodded. "I'll tell you what I know, which isn't everything. I want you to find who hurt him, but I'd prefer not to have Nick's name blackened in the process, so please be discreet with any information I give you."

She'd referred throughout to Nick being *hurt*, but the prospect of him being dead was very real. Given the state she was in it might be best to delay discussing this until they had more evidence.

"Did anyone in the house notice anything unusual this morning? Perhaps someone caught a glimpse of whoever left the, er, item," Harry said.

"It's not an 'item,' as you put it, Inspector. It's my Nick's left hand. It still had his wedding ring on it. You have to find him quickly. He could be lying somewhere, bleeding and in pain."

With these words, she dissolved into tears again.

She recovered herself. "You're right, I'm too upset to go through this today. Speak to Craig, Nick's brother. They run the car showroom together, have done since the start. They usually get on well together, but they've been at loggerheads for months and I've no idea why, Nick wouldn't say. But something was very wrong between them."

"We'll do that," Harry said. "Anyone else we could talk to?"

"Andy Marsh has been giving him a load of grief lately. He's been on the phone, threatening, warning him. Nick laughed it off, said Andy was a fool, but he's not, is he? He's Nick's rival and a killer."

CHAPTER SEVEN

"Do we know where is the Audi, Craig?" Harry asked.

Jess nodded. "The local showroom is on the Ryebridge Road, just before that huge stone church."

"I felt sorry for her back there."

Jess shook her head. "She must know he's most likely dead, but she doesn't want to admit it, does she?"

"It's a very real possibility. And she's not going to take it very well when we have to break the news."

While Harry drove, Jess rang Angela, the team's admin assistant, at the station to get whatever information they had on the brother and the company.

Call over, Harry asked, "What do we know then? Is Craig Sutton a good lad or what?"

"It seems he's the straight one, no record. The business is on the level too. A limited company trading for the last ten years, good reputation and profitable. They have five showrooms in the Greater Manchester area. Nick and Craig run this one together, with managers at the others."

"It has to be a cover for something, and laundering the drugs money is my bet," Harry said. "It's not in Nick's makeup to keep things legal."

"Well, it seems that Craig isn't operating a cover for anything. Perhaps that's what he and Nick had been arguing about," she said.

"We'll see."

"What's going on in that mind of yours?" Jess asked. "Go on, what theories have you got?"

"An argument, a fight, someone ends up dead is one thing. But what's happened to Nick Sutton is way over the top. It smacks of gang warfare to me, a cold-blooded killing, not a spat between brothers. And you know what that means, don't you? Andy Marsh."

But Jess didn't see it. "What would they argue about? I thought that was all sorted. They'd split the local turf, such as it is, between them, and each have their own areas. That way it doesn't get messy and the profits continue to roll in. We might not like it, but it's worked fine for ages. Why start fighting now?"

"Well, it's certainly got messy now, so something went wrong," Harry said. "Remember what Caroline said? I reckon that *something* she mentioned is the Baxendale."

"I'm sure that Marsh and Sutton had other things going on, scams they were involved in. They must have. The Baxendale is a hellhole, so ask yourself, is it, or anything else in Ryebridge for that matter, worth fighting over?"

"We'll see."

The pair pulled up in front of the Sutton car showroom and made for the office.

A young receptionist greeted them with a smile. "Looking for anything in particular?"

Harry smiled back and showed her his warrant card. "Craig Sutton."

The smile turned into a frown. "I'll fetch him."

Jess cast her eyes over the swish reception area and the rows of gleaming vehicles parked outside. "Some set-up. Posh cars too, and a good selection."

"Nothing new though, they're all second-hand," he said.

"Better priced, Harry. A new car depreciates a lot during the first year."

"The young lady is right, which is why we concentrate on the 'nearly new' market. Good quality, in tip-top condition, our customers get an excellent deal."

A smiling Craig Sutton appeared and gestured for them to follow him.

Harry had met both brothers before. Craig was the slighter and shorter of the pair. In fact, they didn't look alike at all. They both lived in Ryebridge and appeared to get along in the main. So, what had gone wrong?

"You'll be here about Nick," Craig said. "I'm still in shock. We had our differences, me and Nick, but I can't believe that anyone would do that to another human being."

Harry had to admit that he did look genuinely cut up about his brother. "Caroline's told you then."

"Yes, this morning. We'd been having a few differences lately, but I have always supported Nick, despite his dubious reputation, so please don't ask me to tell tales on the man. We all know what he is, but he's my older brother and I've always looked up to him. He's a great businessman, started the car sales up from scratch."

"Did any of these differences get ugly?" Harry asked.

"No, not really. We never came to blows or anything, it was all shouting and swearing. He could be difficult to get along with at times, but I've always made allowances. He was my brother — you know, family. It was him that got me into the car business. Best thing I ever did, throwing in my lot with him."

"When did you see your brother last?" Harry asked.

"Three days ago. He left early in the afternoon, said he had someone to meet."

"Did he say who?" asked Jess.

"No, and I didn't ask. He was in a rush as I recall. He didn't say it was important, but he did seem anxious. The tenants had been giving him some aggro. Rents not paid, damage done to the properties, that sort of thing. He'd had a couple of phone calls and I presumed he was going off to sort it."

That was a new one. "Tenants?" Harry asked.

"Well, yes." Craig Sutton seemed surprised that they didn't know. "As well as a half-share in the car sales business, Nick also owns a number of properties that he rents out."

"Where?"

"The Baxendale estate. Years ago, before that estate became the nest of vipers it is today, the council tenants were allowed to buy. Nick bought a few that came up for resale. Currently, he has five in his portfolio."

"Why the Baxendale, Mr Sutton?" Jess asked. "I'm not being funny, but it's not the best place to own property around here."

Craig Sutton nodded. "I did try to tell him, but he'd have none of it. Nick is always right according to him, but he made a mistake there. Those houses have brought him nothing but grief." Craig paused, seeming to consider his next words carefully. "It wouldn't surprise me if one of those bastards did for him."

"Are you thinking of anyone in particular?" Harry asked.

"He's had a lot of dealings with the Cassidy crew lately. They're a bunch of scallies the lot of them, and God knows how many live in that house they rent off him. If they're running true to form, they'll have turned that property into nothing more than a drugs den. I've tried telling Nick, but he never listens to anyone. I know that Martha Cassidy threatened him, not that Nick was scared. He simply laughed it off. Then he goes and gives the woman the contract for servicing the cars here before they're sold on."

Harry could barely believe what he was hearing. The Cassidy family were all troublemakers. Martha's reputation for protecting her family, regardless of what it took, was well-known. "Martha Cassidy looks after the saleroom cars?"

"Yes. Ludicrous, isn't it? They have a car repair workshop. So, when the Cassidys' first invoice comes in, Nick challenges it and gets an ear bashing. They reckoned Nick was trying to short-change them. Ryan Cassidy came round here with that mother of his, and next thing we get a brick thrown at a Volvo we had on show. It smashed the windscreen. Cost us a fortune to replace."

"Did you report it?" Harry asked.

"No. Nick said to let it go, said he'd deal with it himself."

"When was this?" Harry asked.

"Give me a moment and I'll tell you exactly." Craig Sutton looked at his mobile. "Ten days ago, just as we were closing for the day."

"Has Ryan Cassidy or any of that family been back since?" Harry asked.

"No," Craig said "I suppose Nick must've had that word. Mind you, Martha and her brood kept the contract. But we don't send them the same volume of jobs now."

CHAPTER EIGHT

They were back in the car when Harry's mobile rang. It was Dr Melanie Clarke, one of the pathologists from Reid Pathology and Forensics.

"We've had a look at the body part, and I've compiled a preliminary report. There were a couple of interesting findings. Do you want to read my email or come down here and I'll run through them with you?"

It was easier if Melanie explained in person, and they were only minutes away. She could go over the tricky bits he didn't grasp. He could also have a quick word with Hettie. "Give us ten minutes," Harry said. "We need all the pointers we can get." He looked at Jess. "The Reid, they've got something. Okay to make the detour? We'll visit the Baxendale later."

"As long as we don't leave it too late. The Baxendale is no place to be after dark."

Harry laughed. "Afraid of the gremlins that wander the streets?"

"Dunno about gremlins. Druggies more like."

"We'll be fine, trust me. We can see if Kelsey Green is up to a conversation too."

"It's the kid we need to speak to, if that's even possible," Jess said.

"She'll have settled in with her mother now, we might get something."

"You're joking. No kid could settle around Kelsey, the woman's a nightmare. I hope social services are keeping that eye on things like they promised. They do have a reputation for being lax. They reckon they do their best, but they're hampered by inadequate budgets and lack of qualified staff. We know all that but we still allowed that Jackson woman to give Lucy back to her mother."

Harry shook his head. "That wasn't our call, Jess. The social worker made the decision, so it's up to her to ensure Kelsey does the parenting thing right."

Reid Forensics was a purpose-built facility built to offer both post-mortems and forensic investigation services to several police stations across a wide area. It was a two-storey building situated on the far side of Hebbridge as you left the town and headed towards the hills and into West Yorkshire.

Melanie Clarke met them and led the way into the lab. "Hope neither of you are feeling squeamish. Severed body parts aren't everyone's cup of tea."

The hand, which had been cut off just above the wrist, was lying on a table in the mortuary. The macabre sight made Jess shudder. That poor man. Had he been conscious?

"See the ragged edge." Melanie pointed to it. "I think the hand was removed with an electric saw or hedge cutter. The wound has a lot of debris in and around it, there's bruising too."

"Does that suggest he was alive when it was done?" Jess shook her head. "Poor sod."

I'll run further tests, see what we find. But from the congealed blood gathered in the ragged wound, I'd say yes, he was."

"Saw or hedge cutter?" asked Harry. "The stuff of most garden sheds."

"They're certainly easy to get hold of, I have one myself," Melanie said. "Another point to bear in mind, despite what his wife has told you, it would be prudent to make certain of the identity. Nick Sutton's prints are on record so we'll soon know but we'll do DNA tests to be sure."

"His wife is sure it's him. She recognised the ring," Harry said.

"I take it you are looking for the rest of him?" Melanie asked. "If he is indeed dead. The weather is cold at this time of year, but it's warmed up these last couple of days. If the body is out there, perhaps hidden, it won't keep."

"Any clue as to where this might have happened?" Harry asked.

Melanie shook her head. "I'm good, but even I can't work miracles. I've got a hand, that's all. Although I did find oil under the fingernails — dirty oil, the sort you get from an old car engine. Again, we'll run tests."

"That suggests a garage or workshop," Jess said. "That could mean his brother, Craig."

"Then again, it might not. Don't forget the Cassidy clan figure in this too. We'll keep an open mind for now, Jess," Harry said.

"Hi, you two." Standing in the doorway was Hettie Trent. "I'll let you know when the results are in. I'm prioritising the hand, so the shoes will have to take a back seat for now, sorry."

"The kid's home now, so no problem," Jess said.

"Can I have a word?" Harry asked.

Smiling, Jess and Melanie watched him dart off.

* * *

They were on their way back to the car, Harry wearing that familiar daft smile on his face. "She's agreed to come out with me again. Dinner at the Indian restaurant in the square."

"More fool her. I thought Hettie had more sense," Jess said

"We're not going back to mine, so it should be fine." He grinned. "Don and his lady have gone to his parents' for a few days and left me the keys."

"Well, let's hope his housekeeping is better than yours."

"Oh, it is, no worries there. Quite the little housewife is Don."

"Where to now, the Baxendale?" Jess asked.

"We'll make it a quick one. Check in with Kelsey and see if the kid is up to talking to us."

"Don't get your hopes up. According to her mother, she hardly talks at all. But let's get in and out quick. It's getting dark and that place is dangerous."

They pulled up outside the house where Kelsey lived with her small daughter. It was a semi, on a wide street with a large front garden.

"It should be pleasant here," Jess said. "A tree-lined street, plenty of space, and look at the size of the front garden. Kelsey Green is lucky to have a house like this and not one of those dreadful flats in the blocks."

"Except that she's trashed the place," Harry said. "Look at it, even the statement old mattress leaning against the fence, and there's bags of rubbish strewn all over what was once a lawn."

Harry shuddered. Despite the state of his own camper van, seeing how Kelsey had let the place deteriorate creeped him out. Estates like the Baxendale weren't alien to him. He'd lived on one himself for a while, and he knew the dangers. He also knew how hard it was to escape from a background of poverty and deprivation. And if you did, the move wasn't always for the better. The place had caused bad memories to crowd his mind. He needed a distraction.

"Let's get this over with."

They approached the front door. It was growing dark but there were no lights on inside and the curtains were wide open.

"I can't see much, except for Lucy. She's sitting on the rug watching TV," Jess said.

"Kelsey?"

"No sign. You don't think she'd go out and leave Lucy alone, do you?"

"Who knows." Harry banged on the door several times and shouted, but only the child responded, jumping up and looking around her.

"You're scaring her, Harry. Even if Kelsey was asleep, she'd have woken up by now. We have to get inside. That little girl is all on her own."

"Perhaps Kelsey is out the back."

"I'll go round and check, but I'm afraid something's not right."

After a few minutes, Jess let Harry in the front door. "The back door was wide open, and Kelsey looks spark out on the sofa."

While Jess spoke to the little girl, telling her not to be frightened, Harry went to rouse the mother. "She's not asleep, Jess," he whispered. "She's not breathing. I think she's dead."

CHAPTER NINE

Harry rang for an ambulance, which arrived within ten minutes. As they had feared, the paramedics pronounced Kelsey Green dead. Jess took Lucy upstairs while Harry rung Reid Forensics and Rhoda Jackson from child services. Soon, the house was crowded.

"Looks like an overdose to me," he said to Melanie, who had come from the Reid.

She nodded. "There's certainly enough drug paraphernalia lying around. We'll find out exactly what she took, back at the centre."

Upstairs, Jess was doing her best to calm the child, who was upset by the strange voices coming from downstairs. She kept asking for her mummy.

"You're going on a little holiday," Jess told her. "D'you want to choose some things to take with you?"

She seemed to brighten up. "Clara?"

"Sorry, Lucy, but I don't know Clara."

Laughing, Lucy grabbed a soft toy duck. She handed it to Jess saying, "Clara cluck-cluck."

Jess smiled. "Oh, I see. Clara is your special toy."

Lucy giggled. "No. Clara cluck-cluck. Clara not a toy."

Jess shook her head. Well, maybe the little girl believed that Clara was a real duck. She started to pack some of her clothes for her, then picked up another toy. "D'you want to take this dolly too?"

Lucy grabbed the doll and held it close to her chest along with the soft duck. "Mummy?"

The child was barely three. How to tell her? "Your mummy isn't well, sweetheart. But don't worry, you're going to have a nice time."

"Are you ready, Jess?" Harry shouted up the stairs.

She carried Lucy down and handed her to Rhoda Jackson. "I've sorted her some stuff."

Thankfully, Kelsey's body had been taken away. Jess looked at the sofa and shuddered. Poor woman, what had happened to her?

As if reading her thoughts, Harry whispered. "They think it's a massive drug overdose. Look."

A table beside the sofa was covered in white powder and there was a syringe lying on the floor.

"God knows what she took," he said, "but she gave no thought to Lucy's safety while she got off her head."

"I didn't think it would work, Kelsey looking after the child," Rhoda said. "She had no concept of responsibility, that one. I only looked in this afternoon too. I'm afraid we had words. Kelsey resented the fact that she wasn't allowed to speak to the press yet."

"What will happen to Lucy? Does she have other family?"

"No, apart from Kelsey the mite had no one. She'll go to foster parents. She'll be much better off. The family I have in mind are good people and they'll look after her."

"I've put a few things together for her, including a toy she seems to like." Jess handed over the bag. Thankfully, the child seemed quite content, oblivious to her mother's sad fate.

Once Lucy was safely out of the way, Harry took a good look around. "Drug paraphernalia. This place is full of it."

"It's lucky that Lucy didn't pick anything up, try to copy her mother and take the stuff."

"Yeh," Harry said.

Jess was angry at Kelsey's sheer lack of consideration for her child. "Thankfully, I think Lucy was too intent on watching the telly to notice what was happening to her mother."

"Even so, this could so easily have been twice the tragedy it is," Harry said. "Particularly if we hadn't come along when we did."

"The kid is safe, and she'll stay that way now. You should be pleased. She'll be much better off."

"We'll seal the house," Hettie said. "We'll make a start now but most of the forensic work will be done tomorrow morning — orders from the boss. He's decided to take a quick look for himself tonight on his way home. I'll hang on and talk him through it."

The man in charge at the Reid was Professor Hector Steele, a forensic pathologist. What was his interest, Harry wondered? Overdoses were fairly par for the course around here.

"I'll get uniform to watch the place," Harry said.

"I wonder what she took," said Jess.

"A load of the usual crap I expect," Harry said.

"It's a helluva lot by the look of it. Where did she get the money to buy it? And more to the point, who sold it to her?"

"Yes, I get it, Jess," Harry said. "We've got dozens of questions and no answers, but we will have. We'll get the forensics report and deal with it then."

"And meanwhile? What if there's a bad batch doing the rounds? What then, Harry? Do more people have to die before we act?"

"You forget, we have no idea who's doing the dealing on the Baxendale."

"I think we can take a reasonable guess. Andy Marsh and his crew for starters. Who else?"

"So, what d'you want to do? Go bang on his door, drag him down the station? We can question him till we're blue in the face, but we've got nothing that incriminates him. We need solid evidence before we tackle the man. Marsh is wealthy and knows the drill. He'll have alibis oozing from every pore. He'll probably deny even knowing the Baxendale exists."

"You just don't want to miss your hot date with Hettie," Jess said, only half joking.

"I doubt that'll happen now. She'll be tied up with Hector all night."

"Poor you," Jess teased. "But we do need the forensics. With luck we might get prints from those packets scattered on the floor, and then we'll know who sold Kelsey this crap."

Hettie returned to the sitting room from upstairs. "Sorry, Harry, we'll have to put our date on hold. This little lot will take a while. Apart from which, with the prof on his way I need to stay. He'll expect my complete attention."

Jess gave Harry a sympathetic grin.

"Don't you dare say a word," he whispered

CHAPTER TEN

Day Three

The following morning, Jess collared Harry as soon as he entered the main office. "Rodders has been asking for you. He didn't look happy either. What've you been up to?"

"Nowt. I'm a good, clean-living lad, you know that."

But that wasn't the image he presented this morning. "You look rubbish. Grey in the face, scruffy hair . . . another heavy night I'd say. You really do need to rethink the lifestyle, Harry."

There was a lot about Harry Lennox that Jess couldn't work out. He was smart, good at his job, so why did he live the way he did? And why his reluctance to discuss his past? "Why d'you have to drink so much? I know the job is stressful but most of us manage. Your body might cope while you're young but give it a few years and the lifestyle will catch up, mark my words. It always does."

He grabbed a coffee from the machine. "I cope well enough. I drink to get to sleep, that's all."

Jess didn't understand that either. At the end of most days she fell into bed exhausted and slept until her alarm woke her. "Why is that? Bad dreams? Memories? Or that cesspit you're living in?"

"Yeah. Something like that."

Again, no proper answer. Jess had to admit the man intrigued her. They'd been working together for two years now, and she hardly knew any more about him than she did that first day. He was a good detective and always had a wisecrack at the ready. But what lurked underneath the superficial, affable young man? What had his past done to him to make him this way?

"Never mind the coffee, go and see the super," she urged. "And be sharp. Professor Steele wants to see us at the Reid ASAP."

"Popular this morning, aren't we?"

* * *

Harry went along the corridor to Superintendent Roderick Croft's office. "You wanted to see me, sir?"

Roderick Croft looked up from behind his desk. He was a heavyset man in his fifties with greying hair and a ruddy complexion. He was sweating, which accentuated the freckles on his face. He'd spent the last twenty years in the force at Ryebridge and had worked his way up the ladder. He lived in a Cheshire village, had been privately educated and spoke with a plummy accent. The team had nicknamed him 'Rodders' from the off and it had stuck. "We have a problem, Harry. If the stuff collected last night from Kelsey Green's place is anything to go by, then the Baxendale is awash with a new batch of drugs — cocaine cut with fentanyl. I've had Steele on the phone this morning and he's worried. The stuff is strong and deadly. So far, there have been three fatalities including the Green woman."

That was bad news. Harry had a feeling that it wouldn't get any better. "Do we have any intel, sir? Knowing who was supplying it would do for starters."

"Nothing much, but Steele said something interesting. He reckons anyone who knows anything about preparing this stuff would be aware of how lethal it is because of the amount of fentanyl used. This is no money-making scheme, Harry, this is some idiot on a killing spree."

That put a new slant on the dealing. "Not the old contenders then," Harry said. "Given the hand found yesterday, Sutton is presumed dead. That means Marsh has the opportunity to clean up. He stands to make a fortune, so it doesn't make sense for him to kill off all the customers."

"That's what I thought," Rodders said. "Someone new then, with a quite different agenda. What d'you think?"

Harry didn't know what to think, other than they had a lot on their plates — the probable Sutton killing and now this.

"I've allocated a larger than usual uniform presence on the Baxendale estate. They'll keep their ears to the ground, and we'll see what they come up with. Meanwhile, I want you to continue with the Sutton case. We need to determine if the man's dead or not. How are you doing with that? Making any headway? He was a dealer and Marsh still is. Not that we've managed to get the proof we need to put either of them away. If there's the slightest possibility that Marsh is behind what happened to Sutton, perhaps this time we could try harder, get the evidence and make the charges stick." He glared at Harry as if that was down to him alone. "And bear in mind that there could well be a connection between the bad drugs and Sutton's disappearance."

"I've spoken to Caroline and Nick's brother, Craig. We have one or two leads which we'll follow up today, sir."

"I want this wrapping up fast. We cannot have the Baxendale residents dying by the dozen. I want to know who sold that stuff to the Green woman, and I want an update later."

Harry made his way back to the main office. Three deaths including Kelsey Green. If they didn't get on top of this quick, and that stuff was still circulating, there'd be no addicts left on the Baxendale. Or was it just certain addicts being targeted?

The thought stopped him in his tracks. It was a wild idea, but could there be something in it? For now, he decided to file it away in his head under 'possibilities' and keep it to himself.

"You okay?" Jess asked when he returned. "Rodders give you a roasting, or what?"

"No, but he's worried. This drugs thing on the Baxendale is serious. Cocaine cut with a generous helping of fentanyl."

"That's what killed Kelsey?"

"Yep, and two others besides. We'd better get off. Professor Steele is waiting for us."

* * *

Harry didn't say a word during the ride to the Reid. Why kill the punters? The question kept going round in his head. It didn't make sense. Was it a mistake or was it like he'd thought, a deliberate act? But that still didn't make sense. There was too much money to be made in dealing. Kelsey, for one, was a regular user. The whole thing made him uneasy.

"Want to share?" Jess asked.

"No. I'm still trying to add things up."

"What did Rodders want? Sutton or the drugs thing?"

"A bit of both, Jess. The drug problem needs sorting or kids will be dropping like flies and there won't be much we can do."

"Can't we warn them? People have died, we have to do something. Get the press to help, do a TV appeal — anything for God's sake!"

"I'll have a word with Rodders when we get back," Harry said.

Whether that would do any good was debatable. That was a lot of dope in Kelsey's house, and Harry doubted she had the money to pay for it. Someone must have given her the stuff free. If that was the case, there had to be an ulterior motive. But what? Had Kelsey upset someone? Was it connected to her daughter's disappearance? There were just too many questions and no answers.

Professor Hector Steele was waiting for them in the main lab at the Reid Centre. A tall, skinny man with a hooked nose, red hair and a beard, he was a serious individual who didn't talk about much other than his work. Hettie had told Harry that he was a keen fisherman. Harry couldn't see it. All that sitting on a riverbank with nothing but sandwiches and a tin of maggots. Not what he envisaged someone like Steele doing in his spare time at all.

"Kelsey Green was the third victim to be brought in from the Baxendale in the past week," Steele told them. "Drugs were found at all three addresses. I've analysed what was left behind and in all instances the proportion of fentanyl to cocaine was the same. I don't think this was a mistake — some newbie not knowing how to cut the stuff properly — I think it was deliberate."

"Uniform have been questioning the neighbours," Harry confirmed. "One stated that Kelsey was desperate and had been given the drugs by a man she'd not seen before. We all know that isn't how drug dealing goes. The stuff is sold, not doled out like sweets to anyone who asks. According to the neighbour, Kelsey had dozens of little packets stuffed in her pockets."

"Did the neighbour say anything else about this bloke who gave Kelsey the stuff?" Steele asked.

"No. They don't like talking to the police, do they? But we will ask again. When news of the deaths gets round, they might be more willing to tell us something," Harry said.

"A drugs war?" Jess said. "But if that's the case, why give the stuff away?"

"One of the two main players is dead," Harry said. "And given the absence of anyone jumping into his shoes, end of war. That is if the hand did belong to Nick Sutton?" He looked enquiringly at Steele.

"Yes, the prints confirm as much. We're running DNA as there's just a chance we might find a trace of whoever did that to him, but it'll take a little longer."

"Any idea of when he was killed?" Jess asked.

"Don't jump to conclusions, we can't be sure he's dead. He could be being held somewhere, injured, bleeding and in pain. It all depends on whether the stump was attended to or not. As for when the hand was removed, it's tricky to determine," Steele said. "But there's no evidence of the hand being kept in a freezer and decomposition is minimal, so not long."

Someone having a beef with Sutton was one thing, but did it have anything to do with the drugs? "Anything else?" Harry asked.

"Don't forget the hand had oil under the fingernails. It was old, dirty oil, the type you'd get in a garage or mechanic's workshop."

Harry looked at Jess. "We'd better have a word with the Cassidy family, see what they have to say for themselves. Nick and Martha Cassidy had an argument, perhaps it got nasty. Martha does have a reputation."

CHAPTER ELEVEN

The Cassidy clan had a car repair workshop on the Baxendale, and at this time of day that's where they were likely to find Martha. If not, they'd try her home. She didn't live far away, in one of Sutton's houses along with the rest of her brood, near Kelsey Green's place. According to Caroline Sutton, Martha and Nick had had serious issues lately. It was time to find out what had actually gone on.

"Martha Cassidy is a dangerous thug. Want me to organise backup?" Jess asked. "Half her family work in that place of theirs and all of them are huge strapping lads who'll do her bidding without a second thought. I don't know if you've met her, but she's wild, doesn't give a damn about the law."

"I'll take my chances," Harry said.

"I wasn't thinking of you. You're not in this on your own, you know. The idea is that we work together." Why was Jess having to constantly remind him of this? "And I don't fancy having Martha Cassidy punch me one. That woman has a short fuse where her family are concerned. Challenge them, even hint that you suspect them of something illegal and she'll pounce. Ask DC Vance if you have any doubts. That bust nose and broken arm he was sporting a few months ago were down to her."

"So why isn't she under lock and key?" Harry asked.

"No witnesses, no cameras, nothing, just her word against that of Vance. She's brought in and alleges police brutality because a mug of hot tea got spilled over her hand. Her brief had her out in record time with only a caution."

Perhaps she was right, and softly does it was the way to go. Harry had to admit he was inclined to be a bit gung-ho at times, but that was his style. "Anything suspicious, in fact any excuse at all, and we take them all in, get a warrant and have that place of theirs searched from top to bottom."

"She'll kick off before that happens. Things will get nasty and we'll be in danger while we wait for the troops to turn up."

"Don't get so wound up. It'll be fine. We're CID, investigating a possible murder, Cassidy wouldn't dare."

"I admire your confidence, but I can't say I share it. I've just told you what Cassidy and that family of hers are like. You might be happy to take the risk but I'm not. I'm ringing it in, just in case."

"Just give me five minutes to speak to the woman and then we might think again. For now, serious face on," Harry stated.

The Cassidy workshop was in the middle of a row of lockups behind the shops on the Baxendale, in a confined concrete yard with one way in and out. Tall buildings on three sides with little in the way of overlooking windows made it the perfect place to get into big trouble with no witnesses. A fact which wasn't lost on Jess.

They got out of the car and negotiated their way towards the workshop entrance. There were four wrecked cars outside the doorway and the entrance was practically impassable because of the engine parts strewn over the ground.

"Watch yourselves!" someone bellowed from inside. "Scrap man's due anytime so we're having a sort out."

Jess's heart sank. It was a woman speaking and could only be Martha Cassidy herself. Then she appeared, an overweight, heavy-featured woman dressed in oil-stained overalls, her grey hair scraped back in an untidy bun. On seeing the warrant card Harry flashed her way, she rolled up her sleeves and stood with folded arms, blocking the entrance. There was no way to get past her. Seeing her in person, it was obvious why she'd earned her fierce reputation for protecting her family. Her face was like thunder.

Harry made sure she got a good look at the badge before he said politely, "If you've got a minute, we'd like a word, please."

Jess peered inside. In the gloomy interior, she could make out three shapes at the back, working on some vehicle. "Your Ryan here?" she asked.

"He doesn't work here anymore, so if it's him you want, you're wasting your time."

"Got another job, has he?" Harry asked, his tone conversational.

"No idea. Does what he wants our Ryan. Me and his brothers are quite capable of running this place without him."

"We'd like a word about the argument you and Ryan had with Nick Sutton," Harry said.

The sound of that name seemed to throw Martha Cassidy into a rage. She was walking towards them carrying a heavy looking wrench. About a metre from the pair, she passed a metal bench and brought it down hard, making Jess jump. The noise reverberated around the building.

Cassidy shook the wrench in their faces. "What're you saying? Come on, pretty boy, spit it out! What d'you think me and my Ryan's done?"

"We'd like a word, that's all," Jess said. "But if he's not here, perhaps you can tell us what happened." She tried to smile. "You're not in any trouble, we just think you might be able to help."

"Me? Help you lot?" Cassidy sneered. "Bugger off and think yourselves lucky you can still walk."

"Come on, Martha, that's not very nice," Harry said. "We're dealing with a case of serious assault, possibly murder, and your names have come up."

Martha thrust her face to within an inch of Harry's. She was almost purple with rage and breathing fast. For one awful moment, Jess thought she was going to floor him. She glared at him. "Understand this, Mr Detective, me and my boys have done nothing wrong. We haven't hurt anyone, got it? But we could if pushed. All we want is to run this business and keep our heads down, Ryan too these days. He's a good lad, going up in the world. Got himself a nice new house and a girl on his arm." Her rage seemed to lessen when she spoke of her son.

"A quick word, that's all. It's about Nick Sutton," Harry said.

Martha's eyes narrowed. "What's he said? What lies is he spreading about us now?"

"We think he might be dead, Martha," Jess told her. "When did you see him last?"

This took the wind out of her sails. She laid down the wrench. "Not since last week. We do some of the repairs on them cars they sell. We did a Jag which I took back to the showroom and he paid me."

"You didn't argue?"

"No, we barely spoke. We'd 'ad a few words the time before that — he thought the bill was too steep. But we sorted it, came to an agreement. Now piss off. You lot give my place a bad name."

Inside, the light came on under the ramp. The Cassidy brood were working on an expensive looking sports job. "Nice car," Harry said. "You must have a good reputation for the owner to trust you with that."

Martha Cassidy turned her back and walked off, saying over her shoulder, "Last chance. I won't tell you again."

Jess nudged Harry. "It's time to go."

Harry had one last look and then took a quick photo with his mobile. He followed Jess out. He wanted to know who owned that car and what the Cassidys were doing with it.

"It's not a mystery, Harry," Jess said. "It'll be another one from the Sutton showroom."

Nonetheless, from the relative safety of their own car, he rang the station and got Angela, the office admin assistant, to check who it was registered to. The response made him smile.

"The car's Nick Sutton's, not one of those for sale. Now, what's Martha Cassidy doing with a dead man's car?"

"We don't know for sure that he's dead. This lot fix cars for the Suttons' business, so it follows they'll do the family cars too. We have no excuse to search the place."

He nodded at the workshop. "Not yet, but I want to sneak a look at that car."

"Harry, be careful, you know what that family are like."

"This is a murder investigation, no one is going to stand in our way."

"Okay, point taken, but don't wind Martha up. You could get seriously hurt in the argument that follows."

"I'll take my chances."

CHAPTER TWELVE

Surprisingly, Martha Cassidy didn't put up much of an argument.

"That car's here for a service and it's all above board," she told Harry. She went over to a phone on the wall of the workshop, a smug expression on her face. "I'll ring the Sutton house, and if one of them says it's okay for you to look it over, I won't stand in your way. You can search all you like but you'll find nowt."

The two detectives waited for the okay, confident that Caroline would not object. Moments later, Martha reappeared. "One of the boys will get it off the ramp for you. Fill your boots, copper, but be quick about it."

"Why d'you reckon the Suttons use this place for their car repairs?" Jess muttered to Harry when they were out of earshot. "They have large, expensive showrooms. Somehow a backstreet workshop on a rough estate doesn't fit the picture."

"Doesn't, does it? They're up to something."

"Who, this lot or the Suttons?" she asked.

"Both, who knows, but we're going to find out."

One of Martha's sons parked the car in the yard for them.

"We'll see if Angela can help with an address for Ryan. We could do with a word with him," Harry said. "We'll take a look at the car and then if Angela comes up with the goods, we'll pay him a visit next."

"We have no evidence to suggest that Ryan Cassidy or any of his family is involved in what's happened to Sutton," Jess said.

"They do jobs for the Suttons and there was engine oil under the fingernails of that hand. That'll do for now."

Jess was first to climb into the car and rummage around. "It's very tidy. There's nothing in the glove box but I did find this on the dash." She handed Harry a business card.

"Sean Pickford, private investigator. I wonder why Nick needed a PI."

"We'll have to go and ask Mr Pickford, won't we?" Jess said.

"Hang on, where have I heard that name? I wonder if he's related to that PA of Caroline's," Harry said.

"We'll keep it in mind. Anything else?"

"I'll have a quick look in the boot, and we're done."

The boot was empty except for the spare tyre and a jack, wrapped in a cloth and obviously never used.

"It's just a thought but a sample of the oil they use here might be useful. Forensics could compare it with what they got from the hand," Jess said.

Harry took a breath. How would Martha react to that? "All right, I'll give it a go. You wait here. I won't be a minute."

He took a pair of gloves, a couple of small containers and a swab from the boot of their car and went to have another word with Martha.

"Can I take a couple of samples of your oil?" he asked.

"What the 'ell for?"

Harry smiled. "Just for elimination purposes."

She thought for a moment and then shrugged. "Help yourself and then get lost. You lot are becoming a bloody nuisance. We've got work to do."

She watched as Harry put on a pair of nitrile gloves and took a swab from an oily patch on the floor. Next, he helped himself to a sample from a container on a shelf.

"All done," he said.

"Nasty scars on your 'ands," Martha noted. "What happened to you?"

She actually sounded sympathetic. Maybe Martha had the proverbial heart of gold under that hard exterior. "I got injured in a fire a few years ago," he said, showing her his fingers. "I damaged these hauling someone away from the flames. I'm lucky I've still got the use of them. They might not look pretty but that's just the skin grafts."

"Brave lad. Plenty would have given up the force, grabbed some compensation and taken early retirement or summat," she said.

"Not me, Martha. Love the job too much. The moment I was declared fit for duty, I was back at it again." He gave her another smile, time to strike while she was still feeling sorry for him. "Your Ryan. Will you tell me where he lives?"

She looked at him suspiciously. "What d'you want him for? Like I said, he's changed. Ryan's done nowt."

"Please, Martha, it'll make my job easier if you just tell me."

"Okay, but don't let on you got it from me. Orchard Avenue, number ten, off the estate and through the town, back of the park."

The charm had worked again. "Thanks, Martha."

He returned to the car and put the samples safely in the glovebox. "She's a strange one. Okay one minute and ready to stove your head in the next."

"What was she saying to you then?" Jess asked.

"She noticed my hands, wondered what had happened."

"I've often wondered that myself, but you've never said much, only that it was an accident."

"Which it was, and I saved the day. There's no mystery."

CHAPTER THIRTEEN

Orchard Avenue was close to the house Jess was interested in. Her blue eyes travelled speculatively over the passing streets. "What's one of the Cassidys doing round here?" she asked. "Sort of takes the gloss off the area."

"Ryan's got himself a new bird, so he'll be trying to impress."

"Unless it's her place and she's trying to tame him," Jess said. "Either way, I'm not keen on living so close to one of the Cassidys, not with my job."

"Don't tell the neighbours what you do. In fact, take my advice, keep your life close and folk at arm's length."

"Like you do. Anyone would think you were hiding some big, dark secret, Harry Lennox."

He laughed. "Got it in one. Stop digging, Jess, it won't do you any good and it's beginning to grate."

This was how it always was. He'd crack a joke but say nothing enlightening. The more time Jess spent with Harry, the more intrigued she became. Time to change tack. "I'm surprised Martha gave you Ryan's address. What did you do, smile nicely?"

"Something like that. As I said, she saw my hands. She must have felt sorry for me, so I took advantage."

"Bet she wouldn't have given me the information."

He grinned. "Martha just needs handling right, most women do."

Harry in this sort of mood irritated Jess. One day he'd fall flat on his face. She'd put up with his wisecracks and his secretive ways for two years now and it was eating away at her. Why did he have to be such a closed book? What was so wrong in telling people about yourself, your family, where you were brought up? Harry never even spoke about his time in the force before he transferred here. What was he hiding? Jess watched his face as he drove. It gave nothing away. The time had come to make some discreet enquiries of her own. She'd speak to Anthea. If anyone knew about Harry, she must.

* * *

Ryan's house was a pleasant semi on a street of similar properties. As Jess said, not where you'd expect to find one of the Cassidy clan. There was a new car on the drive, nothing ostentatious, a hatchback, and Harry could hear music coming from inside.

"We're in luck. Looks like someone's at home," Jess said.

Harry rapped on the door and stood back.

"Come in! Door's open."

The pair went inside. A young woman, glass of red in hand, smiled at them from the hallway.

"We're celebrating," she slurred. "Wine's in there." She jerked her head. If it's Ryan you're after, I've sent him out to get more booze."

She spun round and, singing to the music, danced her way into the kitchen. "Who are you anyway? You don't look like Ryan's usual crowd."

"We're not, we're police," Jess said.

The woman laughed. "Martha did her best to warn me. She said their Ryan attracted trouble."

"We just want a word, that's all," Harry assured her.

"You're cute," she said, moving in close and stroking his cheek. "Not like any policeman I've ever met."

"Why the celebration?" Jess asked, coming between them.

"Money, love," the woman grinned. "Ryan had a big win on the horses. We intend to make the most of it — first a party and then a holiday somewhere hot."

"Sizable amount was it, this win?" Jess said.

"Big enough to keep Ryan out of trouble for a while. Please you lot, that will." She took another slug of wine. "If you see that family of 'is, not a word — got it? Slightest whiff of money and Martha'll be round here in a flash demanding a share. That woman's a first-class nightmare."

"Adele! What's going on?" A man strode into the kitchen and set down a bag.

"Thought I'd kick off on my own," she said, holding up a wine bottle. "Want some?"

One look at Harry and Jess, and Ryan Cassidy's face fell. "What're you doing here?"

Harry showed him his warrant card. "You've guessed who we are then."

"I'm a bright lad. Know a copper anywhere I would. What d'you want?"

"You had words with Nick Sutton a few days ago, about an invoice we believe. Things got nasty and a car was damaged."

"That wasn't down to me or Ma. As for the invoice, Sutton's a tight bastard, he needed telling. We did a good job and wanted paying right. He saw sense in the end."

"Have you seen Nick in the last couple of days?" Jess asked.

"No reason to. Anyway, I'm taking a back seat in the garage business for a while. Me and Adele here are having a long holiday."

"Win on the horses, she told us." Harry smiled. "Prove that, can you? You know, if it became necessary."

"Not a problem." Ryan returned the smile.

"What about Andy Marsh? Seen much of him?"

Ryan Cassidy looked at Harry, the grin on his face broader now. "Summat's happened, hasn't it? Trouble on that bloody estate, I bet. Nick and Andy have been at each other's throats for years. Been fighting, have they? One of them get hurt?"

"One of them might even have got himself killed," Harry said.

"Nick? So that's why you're so interested in him." He took the glass of wine Adele offered him. "Well, it's nowt to do with me. Why not go and bother Andy instead? See what he's got to say."

CHAPTER FOURTEEN

"Where does Marsh live?" Jess asked once they were back in the car.

"No idea. Somewhere exclusive, posh, with umpteen rooms and staff, I imagine," Harry said. "We'll pay him a visit tomorrow, but we've nothing on him so don't get your hopes up. It's getting late and I fancy visiting that private investigator before we knock off. We'll gather all the information we can from anyone who had dealings with Sutton recently and then go after Marsh."

Jess looked at the card she'd found in Nick Sutton's car. "Pickford must work from home. This address is on an estate at Hurst. I know it because my auntie lives nearby."

"Why would Nick hire a PI d'you imagine?"

"Could be anything — business reasons, checking up on a supplier. Who knows?" Jess said.

"Is that normal? Is that what businessmen do, spy on the people they deal with?" Harry asked. "Doesn't sound right to me."

Jess shook her head. "We're talking about Nick Sutton. He's not exactly your usual businessman, is he? Sutton's a villain who does what he wants."

"I think it's something else, Jess. Call it instinct but I'm sure Nick would have people of his own to check on business associates."

"Well, we're here now, so let's ask him."

A room downstairs at the front of the house had been converted into an office. Framed in the window sat a middle-aged man studying a computer screen and muttering to himself.

He looked up. "Be with you in a minute. The wife usually does my accounts but she's at work and I can't make head nor tail of them." He picked up the phone. "Sorry to keep you but I can't find the invoice in question. Can I ring you back?"

Harry looked at Jess and rolled his eyes.

Pickford finished the call and turned to greet them. "Sorry about that. How can I help?"

Harry flashed his badge. "It's about Nick Sutton," he said. "We found your business card in his car. You were working for him?"

"The work I do for my clients is confidential," Pickford said.

"Nick Sutton is missing, and the circumstances have led us to believe he may even be dead. So, confidential or not, you need to speak to us."

Pickford looked doubtful. "Joan hasn't said anything about that. Are you sure?"

"Are you Joan Pickford's husband?" Jess asked.

"Yes, she's Caroline Sutton's PA. She'd have rung me about something like this."

"Perhaps she forgot," Harry said flippantly. "Now, back to business. When did you last see Nick?"

"At least a month ago. I have little to do with him or his wife. I leave that to Joan."

"Why did Nick Sutton hire you?" Harry asked.

"He didn't. And I'm surprised you're presuming he did on the strength of finding a single business card."

"We found it in his car," Jess said. "And before you lie to us, remember this is possibly a murder enquiry."

Pickford stared at them for a moment, and then sighed. "Okay, Nick did hire me. He suspected Caroline of having an affair and asked me to watch her."

They should have thought of this, Harry said to himself, but he was still surprised, given what Caroline had told him about how close she and Nick were. "And? What did you discover?"

"As it happened, Nick was right, she was seeing someone, but it was hardly serious. I only saw them together once and all they did was go out for a meal. The bloke's name was Bob Armstrong. They met at the Greek restaurant on Deansgate in Manchester. I spoke to the waitress and she told me Armstrong was staying at the Midland nearby and was there on business. I gave Nick a full report a month ago, which was the last time I saw him."

"D'you know if he tackled Caroline about it?"

"According to Joan, Nick was livid, as you would expect, but once he calmed down, him and Caroline talked it through. She assured him it was a silly fling, and nothing had happened other than dinner, which my report backed up, and she swore she would never do anything so stupid again."

"This man, did he have a partner or wife?" Harry asked.

"I've no idea."

"Do you know anything else about him?" Jess asked.

"No, I would have kept an eye on him for a few days longer, checked if he contacted Caroline again, but he flew off to the States, so that was the end of that."

"What did he look like?" Harry asked.

"Average sort of bloke, there was nothing special about him that I could see."

"Mr Pickford, did you take any photos of the two of them together?" Jess asked.

"Yes, I did take a few. I emailed them to Nick, and then he insisted I delete them completely, which I did."

"We'll speak to Caroline, see if we can access them, or she might have one that she took," Jess said.

"Thank you very much for your help," Harry said. "If we have any other questions, we'll be in touch."

"You know where I am," Pickford said and turned back to his invoices.

* * *

Back in the car, Harry seemed preoccupied. Jess nudged him. "So, Caroline lied to you, said her and Nick were solid. Get over it."

"Why though? It could be important. She should have said something. It makes me wonder what else she's lied about. We have no idea what went on, how Nick really reacted to finding out about Caroline's affair. For all we know, that's what's at the bottom of this."

"Pickford said the bloke was average, ordinary. That doesn't sound like someone who'd kill just to chance his arm with a woman again."

"We don't know that for sure. We need another word with the lovely Caroline."

CHAPTER FIFTEEN

Day Four

First thing the following morning, Harry and Jess went to speak to Caroline. This time they intended to push her about the affair.

"I know you want answers, but we should tread carefully," Jess said to Harry. "If we barge in, upset the woman, we'll get nothing."

"Do you really think a spurned lover did for Nick, 'cause I don't, Jess. Look what was done to him. Whoever took him had a score to settle. If Nick had tackled that man Armstrong, there'd have been a scuffle, one of them would have got their eye blacked, but chopping off a hand, possibly murdering the other, that's something else."

Before they made it to the front door, Harry's mobile rang.

"Long time no speak, laddie, how're you doing? I've been worried."

This was out of the blue and Harry was momentarily thrown. "Sandy? Sorry, I can't talk now, I'm on a case."

"I could do with a chat when you're free. You've not been in touch like you promised. That wasn't our agreement. You said you'd ring every month at least."

Hearing the familiar Scottish lilt brought on a surge of homesickness. He'd love to see Sandy, even if it was just a flying visit, but it wasn't that simple. "Sorry. Time flies and the job is full on."

"You have folk up here who care about you, laddie, never forget that. Your Morag never lets up. She wants you to come back for a holiday."

"You know I can't do that, Sandy, it's too soon. Tell Morag I was asking after her."

"It's been three years," Sandy said. "When you get a minute, she'd love you to ring her. Think you can promise to do that at least?"

Sandy made it sound so simple, but it wasn't. Seeing his old friend after all this time and after what had happened would be hard. There'd be the inevitable questions, the reminiscences, but he knew Sandy, he wouldn't give up. He'd contacted him once and he'd do so again until he got his own way. "I'll ring home at the weekend, cross my heart," he said finally, and ended the call.

Harry turned to Jess, who was hovering at his shoulder. "Personal stuff, sorry."

"Who's Sandy and Morag?" she asked.

"Just people I know. They're nothing to do with the case."

"From back home?"

He didn't reply.

"And why's it too soon? Too soon for what?"

"Leave it, Jess," he said sharply.

He didn't have time for Jess's prying right now. Sandy was right, he had neglected his old friends and family. But he wasn't ready to deal with it, not yet. Hearing Sandy's voice, that soft Scottish burr so warm and comforting, had made him think of home. There were times when he wished . . . But he'd had no choice and like it or not, he had to live with it. He shook himself and faced the door.

Joan Pickford let them in and led the way through to the sitting room, where Caroline looked up hopefully.

"You have news?" she asked.

Harry came straight to the point. "Why didn't you tell us about the man you were seeing, this Bob Armstrong? Given what's happened, that's a serious omission."

She stared at them for a moment and then turned away. "Yes, I should have, but it's something I'm trying to forget. I acted foolishly. I can't believe I came so close to cheating on Nick."

"He found out. He must have been mad," Harry said.

"And then some," Caroline said with a wry smile. "He hit the roof, ranted for hours about what I'd done and what he'd do to Bob if he ever got his hands on him."

"And did he?"

"No, fortunately Bob wasn't around. The day after we went to that restaurant he had to leave for the States — a business problem that needed his immediate attention. It gave me time to think and I rang him later and called a stop to the whole silly business. By the time Nick found out about us, Bob was well out of the way and had most likely forgotten all about me."

"Nick did nothing about it?"

"No, he didn't, other than have a go at me. Frustrating for him, I imagine, but the man wasn't in the country and Nick wasn't about to chase after him all the way to the States. Instead, he had a moody couple of days until he got over it and eventually saw the episode for what it was, a silly mistake."

"You had one date with the man? That's all?" Harry said.

"Yes."

"When was this?" Harry asked.

"About four weeks ago."

"Do you have a photo of him?"

"I did, but Nick made me delete it off my phone. It was no big deal. Me and Bob didn't have a future."

"Why did Nick hire a private investigator? What aroused his suspicions?"

"Bob and I only met the once, but we'd chatted via text. Nick must have seen some of our messages on my mobile. I wasn't careful enough, left it lying around and it has no passcode."

"Was there anything compromising in them?" Jess asked.

"No, but the fact that I was messaging a man Nick didn't know was enough. He's very possessive."

Harry nodded. Caroline's story was plausible enough. But his head was elsewhere, his thoughts kept straying to his past. Sandy's call had thrown him, put him off stride and brought back all the bad memories. He'd left his previous life out of necessity. An old enemy he'd crossed swords with on a case in Glasgow believed him to be dead, and Harry wanted to keep it that way. Return, even for a short visit, and word would soon spread.

"There's no chance that what happened to Nick is down to this Bob fella?" Jess asked, glancing at Harry.

"No, he's still in New York," Caroline said, "and won't be back for a while. I do get the odd message from him."

Harry shook himself. This needed his attention. "We're going to need his full name and phone number. He'll have to be checked out," he said.

CHAPTER SIXTEEN

Back at the station, Harry set Angela on the job of finding out more about Bob Armstrong and where he'd spent the last month.

"Harry!" It was the super. "The disappearance of the Green child, I've got Maxwell's team looking at it again. Someone took her, and given she's back safe, I doubt that was Sykes. That leaves you clear to concentrate on the drugs situation and the Sutton case. I know that's pushing it, but given it's Sutton who's involved, the two are most likely linked. Have you got anything yet?"

"One or two leads but nothing that's led anywhere yet, sir."

Superintendent Roderick Croft scoured the incident board, frowning. "Chase up forensics. Don't let them drag their feet on this."

Once he'd left the office, Harry turned to Angela. "Has anything come in from the Reid?"

"Nothing on the system yet," she said.

"Are you happy with him passing on Lucy's disappearance to Maxwell?" Jess asked.

"What choice do I have? Anyway, we've got enough on as it is." Harry looked over to where young PC Carter was having his lunch. "Was anything found on that path where the kid's shoes turned up?"

"We got tyre tracks from an SUV. There's a camera a few metres away and one by the gate. We've had some of the footage through, and we'll go over it."

"Make it a priority. Have moulds of the tracks been taken?"

"Yes, sir, the bods from the Reid were straight on it."

"Speaking of which, want to take a ride over to the Reid, see what Hettie is working on?" Jess asked. "She might have something that's not hit the system yet."

Harry nodded. They had nothing else to do. All the leads they'd followed so far had led them nowhere. Caroline had given them a plausible answer and it didn't appear that the private investigator was involved. What Harry really wanted to know was whether the disappearance of Nick Sutton had anything to do with the deadly drugs being doled out on the Baxendale.

* * *

"Kelsey Green's body yielded nothing other than what we expected," Hettie said. "She died from a massive overdose of fentanyl. The plastic bags the stuff was in are another story, however. They are covered in prints, but only one other set apart from Kelsey's."

Harry waited for the revelation. Now they would find out which of the Baxendale dealers was selling the lethal stuff.

"Not on the database, I'm afraid."

That was a mega disappointment. So much for the revelation, and no prints on record meant this had to be down to someone new. Is that what had happened? Some new face had muscled in, killed Sutton and taken over his patch? Yet there had been no intel, no whispers that suggested such a development.

"You sure?" Harry asked.

70

"Quite sure. Whoever is selling or giving this stuff away is new or has managed to evade the law up to now. The only positive I can throw into the mix is that we haven't had any more bodies."

Small consolation for another dead end.

"But there is something." Hettie smiled. "Nick Sutton's hand — as I said, there was a deal of debris around the wound. I analysed it and found traces of flesh from elsewhere."

"Are you saying the cutter was used to cut up other parts of his body? That he was dismembered?" Harry asked. "Or do you think what you found belongs to someone else?"

"It looks that way. DNA will prove the theory but I was able to get a small blood trace from the flesh and it's not the same group as the hand."

"What? Someone is chopping people to bits?" asked Jess, a look of horror on her face.

"Well, keep it in mind. We'll know more once the results are through."

"Not something we've met before," Harry said. "Murder, yes, but this is something else." He looked at Jess. "We need to find Nick Sutton, dead or alive."

"We've got officers on the Baxendale and we've checked all his recent contacts. Without something to go on, finding him is a matter of luck, I'm afraid," she said.

"There's still someone we haven't spoken to," Harry said. "I know I've been putting this off, but I think it's time we paid Andy Marsh a visit."

CHAPTER SEVENTEEN

Like Sutton, Andy Marsh also ran a legitimate business. He owned a clothing factory on the Ryebridge industrial site that produced cheap goods which were mostly sold online and by market traders. His wife, Lisa, had a jewellery shop in the town.

"I've rung Marsh's office at the factory but he's not there," Jess said. "The answer machine kicked in, saying the place was closed today. Odd that. You have to wonder why."

"Okay, Lisa it is then. We'll try the Ryebridge shop," Harry said. "We pay her a casual visit without ruffling any feathers and see if she knows or has heard anything about Nick."

"We'll be lucky to get a straight answer. Lisa Marsh is a piece of work, every bit as twisted as her old man. If Marsh is at the bottom of this, she'll back him to the hilt. We have nothing concrete to go on, so, like you say, Harry, gently does it."

He nodded.

"We've examined every other lead and come up with nothing. This has to be what it looks like, a turf war between Sutton and Marsh. Nothing else makes sense."

Harry wanted to agree with Jess, but he had a feeling that it wasn't so simple. He wanted the forensics on that cutter, when they found it, before accepting the possibility.

"Do we know if uniform have picked up on anything untoward on the Baxendale?" he asked her.

"As far as we know, there's been no more lethal stuff doing the rounds. But the addicts are still getting their fix. That, I presume, is down to Marsh and his mob."

They drove into Ryebridge centre and parked the car in the multi-storey. Ryebridge wasn't a large town but it was big enough to have an indoor shopping mall, a market hall and the high street. Not so long ago the shops had been busy, the town vibrant, but today a number of them were empty and boarded up. The jewellery shop owned by Lisa Marsh was in the mall, at the opposite end to the café the pair liked.

"I'm not looking forward to this," Jess admitted as they took the escalator down to the ground floor. "I've met them both before. He's quite the gentleman — all put on of course — but she's as common as muck and doesn't care who she upsets."

"We ask a few questions, keep it simple, it'll be fine," Harry said.

The shop was spacious, with lighting that drew attention to the glittering cabinets full of modern jewellery around the walls. Lisa Marsh spotted them as soon as they walked in. She was tall and skinny, with blonde wavy hair pulled into a ponytail, and wearing a short dress and heels. Andy Marsh was in his fifties, and Lisa must have been at least twenty years younger. Second wife? Harry wondered.

Harry expected a mouthful, to hear the usual insults and be told to leave, but Lisa Marsh surprised him. She gave him a tentative smile and said, "please tell me you've found him."

"Found who, Lisa?" Jess asked.

The woman's dark eyes flashed at her. "My husband of course, idiot! He's been missing for twenty-four hours now and that's completely out of character. Andy doesn't do missing, he likes me and his home life too much."

First Sutton and now Marsh. This was too much of a coincidence. Harry gave Jess a gentle nudge — he didn't want her saying anything about Nick Sutton, not yet.

"Why didn't you contact us?" Jess asked.

"Because you're useless! You're not interested in finding Andy. I expect you're all silently cheering because he's disappeared."

"When did you last see him?" Harry asked.

"The night before last. He went out on a bit of business and never returned. I rang his mobile, it's dead. I rang round his usual haunts, his friends, no one had seen him."

"Factory business, was it? Who else was involved?" Harry said.

She folded her arms and turned away. "It had nothing to do with the factory. He's sorted that one. This was some bloke from the estate I think."

"The Baxendale?"

Lisa nodded.

"This bloke — have a name, does he?" Harry asked.

"I've no idea who he is — someone new. He rang Andy and suggested a meet. I heard Andy shout at him, calling him names. From the little I heard it sounded as if this new bloke had ambitions regarding the estate and Andy wasn't having it." She shrugged. "Whatever was said, he wasn't happy, and he left the house all fired up."

"I bet he didn't like it. Most of his income is tied up in that estate," Harry said.

She glared at Harry. "Look, we run a legitimate business here and at the factory. This is no time to get picky about the type of man my Andy is. He and Sutton make sure this town stays quiet and no one gets too ambitious. They put a stop to a lot of trouble you lot never even hear about. We all know what's what. But now he's missing, possibly in danger, and I want him found."

That was straightforward enough, and Lisa was right. "Okay," Harry said, "this is what will happen. I want you to close up shop, come down to the station and give us a statement. If we're to find him, we need all the information you can give us."

Lisa gave both detectives a dubious look. "Me? Come down to the station? Can't we do it here? Andy has a lot of friends who won't take kindly to me hopping into bed with the police."

He glared at her. "Bottom line, Lisa, d'you want your husband found or not?" She nodded. "Right, we need a blow-by-blow account of Andy's movements over the last week or so, where he went and who he spoke to. That's best done in a quiet environment where you can think straight. And this shop isn't it."

"You're scaring me now. You know something, I can see it in your face. What aren't you telling me?"

Harry sighed. "Just do as I ask, please, Lisa. We all want the same thing here, to find Andy. Okay?"

CHAPTER EIGHTEEN

Lisa Marsh waited in a soft interview room with a woman PC for company while Harry and Jess were in the incident room discussing how much to tell her.

"The minimum," Harry insisted. "I've sent a couple of PCs round to the Marsh house to keep watch and have a look around. We'll visit the factory later."

"Do we tell her Nick Sutton is missing?" Jess asked.

"Missing, but that's it. The woman is wired enough as it is, we tell her what happened to Sutton and she could lose it. For all we know, Marsh will turn up later with some excuse for his absence."

"We tell her Nick is missing, she'll merely shrug and say, so what," Jess said. "I think she should know the truth. That way she might tell us what Marsh was really up to recently and not lead us down a blind alley."

But before Harry had time to reply, his mobile rang. It was PC Carter, one of the two uniforms he'd sent to the Marsh house.

"We've got . . . something, sir," he said. His voice wavered.

It was bad. The young PC was obviously upset.

"It must have been left on the step earlier, but I reckon a fox or something dragged it off before the occupants were even up. The gardener found it in the shrubbery. Sorry, it's a bit mangled and bloody. I think the beast must have had some of it for breakfast."

Harry groaned. He knew what was coming next.

"It's a hand, sir, like with Sutton, cut off at the wrist."

Harry finished the call and looked at Jess. "This changes things. A hand was delivered to the Marsh house earlier today. It wasn't spotted before because it was taken from the step by wildlife."

"Oh no!" Jess exclaimed. "That's making me feel sick. As if cutting off a hand wasn't bad enough . . . What do we tell Lisa now?"

"Given what's happened, it'll have to be the truth. She needs to know the danger her husband is in, and that there is a possibility that he's dead. That way, if she does know anything, she'll tell us."

* * *

Harry gave Lisa the news. She broke down, weeping inconsolably on the PC's shoulder.

"Why my Andy? I don't understand," she said after a while. "Everything was going so well."

"What do you mean, Lisa? Everything with what?" Harry asked.

"Us, the businesses, what d'you think?" she glared at him through her tears.

"When we spoke in the shop we asked about the factory, and you said that was all sorted now. What was sorted?" Jess asked.

"That was just a something and a nothing," she said. "Some stranger made Andy a ridiculous offer for the factory, and said he should think carefully before he refused."

"Does he have a name, this stranger?" Harry asked.

"Andy's PA, Babs Milton, at the factory office will have the details. I've no idea who he was, some chancer probably. Nothing came of it anyway. Andy has no intention of selling up, not yet."

"What about the other business, the dealing and the rest?" Harry asked. "You must understand that we need to know everything and anything that could help us find who hurt your husband, Lisa. Who Andy went off to see the night he disappeared will do for starters."

"He didn't tell me," she wailed. "He never tells me much about that aspect of things. He says the less I know, the less I can tell you lot."

That was all very well but it didn't help. "Had anyone given him any trouble lately? Had he received any threatening phone calls?"

"Nick Sutton was a permanent pain. They'd been arguing again, even came to blows in the pub a couple of weeks ago. He argued with that Ryan Cassidy too. He came into the shop and they went into the back office. Ryan was screaming at Andy. I heard a little but not much. When they'd finished, Ryan went off in a rush. I could see Andy was upset, but he wouldn't tell me why."

Ryan Cassidy again. Too much of a coincidence. "Did Andy talk to Nick Sutton?"

Lisa gave him a look full of scorn. "You know very well they were rivals. They hated each other, always have done. Nick is a piece of cheating scum. Apart from making sure the town stayed quiet, which suited them both, Andy would have nothing to do with him. Have you spoken to Nick? It wouldn't surprise me if he wasn't at the bottom of this. He's threatened Andy with violence many times."

"But they had come to an arrangement — about the Baxendale in particular," Harry said. "And it worked too, up to a point."

"Nothing to do with me," she said. "I'm only interested in the jewellery business. Whatever else Andy gets up to is his affair."

This wasn't helping anyone. "I suspect it's the *whatever else* that's got him into this mess, Lisa," he said.

"You should drag Nick Sutton down here and make him tell you what he's done to my Andy. He'll be at the bottom of this."

She sounded so sure that it was a shame to burst her bubble.

"Not Nick, Lisa, not this time," Harry said gently.

She stared at him, her eyes wide, fearful. "What d'you mean? You don't think Nick did this? Why not?"

"Because whatever has happened to Andy happened to Nick too. He is missing and has been mutilated in the same way."

Her face was a picture as she tried to work this out.

"It follows that whoever hurt your husband, it wasn't Nick, he said slowly. So, I need to know, apart from Nick Sutton, who hated him enough to do that."

"I   I can't think of anyone else. There is only Nick. There was the odd argument with Ryan and his clan, but Ryan's just a hothead, he hits the roof but calms down just as quick. The row the other day was about the dealing, I think. When Ryan came to the shop, he was angry about a bad batch, I heard that much."

The fentanyl! They needed another word with the Cassidy family.

"When Andy went out, did he take his car?" Jess asked.

"Yes, and he had his phone, but that's dead now. And you lot haven't found his car either, have you?"

Jess shook her head. So far they only had Nick Sutton's. "We'll find out when Andy's mobile was last used. I'll need his provider details. Meanwhile, I want you to write down every little detail you remember. The PC here will stay with you. Once you're done, we'll take you home and arrange for a family liaison officer to be with you."

CHAPTER NINETEEN

"Martha won't like it," Jess said with a grin, "you bothering her best boy. And you're driving way too fast. At this rate we'll be lucky to make it to Ryan's house in one piece."

Harry gripped the steering wheel tight. "He lied, the toerag." As if they didn't have enough to think about.

"He just didn't tell us the whole story. There's a difference, you know."

"I just wish we knew what we were dealing with. If there are two bodies out there, they need finding. Perhaps then forensics could give us something useful."

Harry pulled up outside Ryan's house and hammered on the front door. Adele answered. She didn't look pleased to see them.

"What now? Thought we'd sorted you lot." She moved aside to let them through. "Ryan, love, it's the coppers again!" she shouted up the stairs. "He's sleeping it off. Silly bastard drank too much this afternoon."

It was some time before a tousled Ryan Cassidy appeared at the top of the stairway. He yawned, stretched, and demanded water from Adele. "Can't drink booze in the day, never could. What d'you want now?"

"You went to Marsh's shop. You and Andy argued, what about?" Harry said.

Ryan shrugged. "Nowt much, the man's got a short fuse."

Harry shook his head. "Try again, Ryan. Lisa heard some of the conversation, so don't bother lying."

"Oh? And what did she tell you? Not much I bet. She wouldn't dare — wife or not, Andy would kill her."

"Andy's missing, possibly dead, just like Nick Sutton, so what did you discuss?" Harry said.

That shook him up. "Okay, it was about a bit of business on the Baxendale."

"Drugs?" Harry said.

"I know how this works. I say yes and you'll arrest me. Get me banged up for dealing."

"That won't happen, not by me anyway," Harry said. "I just want to know what you argued about."

Ryan heaved a sigh and ran a hand through his untidy hair. "There's been some lethal stuff circulating — well, you know that, you've got the bodies. I thought it was down to Andy, but he said it wasn't and I should talk to Nick. I don't know now, perhaps neither of them were involved."

And that would give them a much bigger problem, Harry thought, an outfit they knew nothing about. "Have you heard anything on the street?" he asked.

"No, but there's someone new dishing out dope to the kids. A foreign guy, big and angry looking. Maybe he's working for himself, I dunno."

Harry gave him a quizzical look. That wasn't how the dealing worked. "You know something, you tell me now, Ryan. We've got three bodies from the Baxendale and I don't want any more."

"I know that, I can count and I'm not stupid," Ryan retorted. "Something's going on but I don't know what." He scratched the stubble on his chin. "That's all I can tell you. You're wasting your time questioning me any more."

81

They were obviously not going to get any more from Ryan. "If anyone mentions names, you come to me, got that?" Harry said. "That way you might avoid a prison sentence. Do you understand, Ryan?"

He nodded.

"Good. Let me down and I'll throw the book at you," Harry said.

"Where to next?" Jess asked as the door closed behind them.

Harry checked the time on his mobile. Marsh's factory would be closing about now, so they'd visit in the morning. "Another word with Caroline. Check if she's remembered anything else since we last spoke. I'd also like to know why she felt the need to cheat on Nick."

"She didn't though, did she? She bottled it and then the bloke left the country," Jess said.

Harry frowned. "That raises the question of what would have happened if the circumstances had been different. While I drive, would you check with Angela if the alibi Caroline gave for him checks out?"

* * *

Caroline Sutton was not happy to see the two detectives on her doorstep again, particularly when Harry brought up Bob Armstrong. "I've already told you about him," she said. "There's nothing I can add."

Jess nudged Harry and showed him her mobile screen. She'd just received a text from Angela at the station confirming that Armstrong had left for the USA when Caroline had said, and he hadn't returned.

"What intrigues me," Harry began, "is why you would feel the need to stray in the first place. You told us you and Nick were happy. So why another man? I don't understand."

Caroline hesitated. "What I told you was the truth, but there were cracks, and as the years went by, the deeper they became." She dabbed at her eyes. "I was stupid, but I was grasping at an opportunity."

"Sorry, Caroline, I'm not with you. What are you getting at exactly?" Harry asked.

"Have you got kids, Inspector?"

Harry smiled. "God no, I'm barely grown up myself."

"Nick and I have none, and that has always been a problem for me. I really wanted children — two would have been perfect, one of each. But Nick was infertile, but it didn't stop me longing for a child. A couple we know were in a similar situation, turned out that the infertility wasn't as complete as they thought. They now have a handsome boy. That gave me hope."

The penny dropped. "You were hoping to get pregnant?" Harry asked. It was a bit extreme, but he supposed it was that biological clock ticking.

"Put simply, yes," Caroline said. "If I was lucky enough to become pregnant, I'd pass it off as Nick's. Given our friend's experience, he'd believe me."

"But he found out about Armstrong and that put paid to your plans?" Jess said.

"Very much so. Now it looks as if I've lost Nick *and* any chance of having a child."

CHAPTER TWENTY

Day Five

First thing the following morning, Harry and Jess met at the shopping mall café to discuss the case over breakfast.

"I feel sorry for her now," Jess admitted. "Fancy wanting kids when your husband is dead set against it. Must have done her head in. I'm not surprised she found another bloke."

"Yeah, but was it a motive to kill him?" Harry asked thoughtfully.

"No. I doubt she's capable."

"This morning we'll visit the factory," Harry said. "Speak to that Babs person, see what's going on there and what instructions Nick left, if any." He paused. "Are you listening at all?"

"You've practically eaten the entire menu," Jess said.

He shrugged. "Missed my meal last night. Chippy was shut and I've no cooking facilities."

"You really do need to get sorted, Harry. You can't continue like this. Your clothes look tatty, you're living on junk food and I bet Don's getting fed up of having that eyesore on his drive."

"He's driven all over Europe in that 'eyesore,' as you call it," he said.

"It looks like it an' all. Get a grip, Harry, sort a flat or better yet, think about buying a house."

"I don't know if I'll stay around that long. I'm easily bored." He yawned as if to emphasise his words.

Jess gave him a long, hard look. That wasn't the real reason, she was certain. It seemed to her that he was constantly on the move because he was hiding something. Jess resolved that when she had a moment, she would find out what it was. She needed to have that chat with Anthea.

"That factory of Marsh's must be doing good business," she said, "They sell to a number of online stores, the cheaper end mostly. They sell a wide range of stuff, very enterprising. They have to be giving the high street a run for their money."

"Motive, d'you think?" Harry asked. "Some irate dress shop owner who wants their trade back."

"Now you're being stupid."

* * *

Ryebridge Industrial Estate was a large rambling mix of workshops and small factories. Andy Marsh owned the biggest property with ample parking and a large loading bay.

"The office is at the side over there," Jess said, pointing. "Believe it or not I came here for a holiday job once, many moons ago when I was a student. I remember the woman who interviewed me was a right tartar. Sent me packing with a mouthful of obscenities and told me not to come back. Scared me stiff, she did. Put me off working big style."

"Didn't you have an appointment?" Harry asked.

"No, I thought I'd simply try my luck."

Harry parked up and looked at the building. "You rang yesterday, shut you said, looks like we're out of luck today as well."

Jess got out of the car and tried the office door. It was locked tight, as was the main factory entrance and the loading bay. "I wonder if this is down to Lisa?"

"I'll ring and ask her. Odd though, they must have plenty of work on with that website to feed." Harry tapped in Lisa's number, but she didn't pick up. "Answerphone. She must be busy in the shop. Let's have a look round, see if we can find a security guard or someone."

Beckoning for Jess to follow him, he walked around to the back of the building. "There's a door here, but again it's locked up tight." He banged on it hard, but no one answered.

"Odd this. It's a weekday, you'd think there'd be someone here, even if the boss isn't around. This place should be going at full pelt," Jess said. "And no Lisa, she's not even answering her mobile."

But Harry wasn't listening. He was on the phone to the station, talking to Angela. "I've got the address of Babs Milton, Andy's PA. Let's see if she knows what's going on."

CHAPTER TWENTY-ONE

Babs Milton lived on the B... not far from Kelsey Green's place. But unlike the tip Kelsey had lived in, Babs's house was as neat as a new pin.

"I knew there was summat up first thing this morning when I couldn't get in." She reached for a sheet of paper lying on the coffee table. "This was pinned to the main factory doors. Seems Andy's sold the place — stupid bastard never said a word. There were forty of us working for him in that factory, good machinists too, and now every last one of us is out of work. I don't know what Andy was thinking of."

Harry took the printed sheet and studied it. Short, simple and harsh. The factory had new owners and the services of all the present staff were no longer required. "Have you told Lisa?"

"I rang, but got no answer, so I texted but I've had nothing back so far. I've also tried Andy, but his phone's dead too."

"I'll have to take this, it's evidence," Harry said. Before popping the sheet in an evidence bag, he took a photograph of it with his mobile. "By the way, Andy Marsh is missing."

"Missing? Andy? I don't get it, unless he's suffering from a guilty conscience. Something's not right. Me and Andy, we have an understanding. I keep that place running like clockwork, stand for no nonsense. We turn out the goods, get them modelled, photographed and onto the website. We're good, and we work hard. Andy wouldn't just walk away without speaking to me, neither would he just sell on a whim."

"The business was profitable?" Jess asked.

Babs waggled her hand. "So-so. In my opinion we sold too cheap. Some months we'd struggle to pay the bills. I know it really pissed Lisa off, she was constantly urging him to produce the more upmarket stuff and sell to the shops."

"But Andy didn't agree?" Jess asked.

"No, he was convinced that producing volume and selling cheap was the way to go. He wasn't in the habit of taking advice from Lisa or anyone else."

"Has he said anything to you about selling in the last few weeks?" Jess continued.

"No, but there's this bloke been sniffing about — coming to the factory, demanding to speak to Andy. Got on his nerves he did, always turning up unannounced. But I can't believe that Andy would cave in and sell to him. The idea is ludicrous." Babs made a face. "Have you met Andy? He's not a man you pester, believe me."

"Do you know who this stranger is?"

"No, but I do know that the offer he made for the place was laughable."

"Could you describe him?" Jess asked.

"He was a big bloke, ugly, and he may have been foreign. There was something about his accent, it certainly wasn't local."

"Okay, thanks, Babs, we'll probably need to talk to you again," Jess said.

Once they were back in the car, Harry said, "We need to speak to Lisa. See if she knows what happened at the factory."

"The shop?"

"Yeah, okay."

* * *

They parked in the multi-storey and while they were on their way down, Harry's mobile rang. It was Hettie from the Reid.

"I've got a result from the analysis we did of the debris found on Nick Sutton's severed hand. Want to come in and discuss it?"

"We're on our way to have a word with Lisa Marsh right now, Hettie. We'll be with you straight after."

"At last," Jess said. "Let's hope she has something we can use."

Harry half expected Lisa's jewellery shop to be closed but it wasn't. "You're not answering calls," he said as they walked through the door. "Is there a reason for that?"

"I'm scared, that's why. My nerves are shot. All the time I'm terrified you lot will ring to say you've found my Andy and I can't bear it."

"We wouldn't ring," Harry said gently. "We wouldn't do that to you, we'd come in person. Anyway, we haven't found him yet, so he may still be alive. Don't give up hope, Lisa."

She nodded, giving him a weak smile. "So, what d'you want then?"

"D'you know about the factory?" he asked.

She looked at them, her eyes wide. "What's happened? Not trouble with the machinists? I couldn't cope, not right now. Babs will have to deal with it."

"Babs tried to ring you. The factory has been sold. It's locked up and this was left on the main doors," He showed her his phone with the image of the printed sheet.

Lisa seemed genuinely puzzled. "This isn't right. Andy would never sell."

"D'you know who was looking to buy the place?"

"There was a man, mithered Andy for weeks about selling to him, but he kept refusing. In the end he got angry and had security throw him out." Lisa looked at the image again. "Give me a moment. I'm going to ring our solicitors."

She disappeared into the back room. When she reappeared, Lisa Marsh was as white as a sheet.

"It's true, the factory's gone. Sold for the princely sum of one pound to a company called 'Lancashire Holdings.' Andy signed the transfer of shares agreement and our solicitor has the paperwork. He confirms that it is his signature, witnessed as well, and by Nick Sutton of all people. There's nothing I can do." She stared at them. "This is what got him taken, isn't it, and why they did that . . . thing to him. They hurt him to make him sign that document."

CHAPTER TWENTY-TWO

"She might be right," Jess said as Harry drove them to the Reid. "Marsh is tortured and made to sign the business over."

Harry shook his head. "It's a reasonable business, makes money some of the time but it's hardly worth killing for. It's a helluva risk to take, and I don't understand why they'd want it that bad. And who are Lancashire Holdings anyway?"

"I'm on it," she said. "D'you know, I hate surfing on my phone. I can never find what I want. I'll have a proper look on the Companies House website when I get back to the station."

"I don't know the name," Harry said. "It certainly gives nothing away. What's bothering me is first Nick and now Andy, and the same method with both. They want the factory from Andy, but what do they want from Nick? Any ideas?"

"Not the car business. I'm sure Craig would have said something if that was the case," Jess said.

"That just leaves the houses on the estate. What d'you reckon?" Harry said.

"A bunch of rundown properties on the worst estate around. Surely no one would want them," Jess said.

"How many properties are there?" Harry asked.

"Five I think, I'll check later."

"Let's see what Hettie's come up with and go from there," he said.

Dr Hettie Trent greeted them with a smile. "The traces of blood and flesh on Sutton's cut hand were from a variety of sources, one of them being Andy Marsh."

So, the killer had used the same tool on both. Perhaps he even had them imprisoned together. "Who else?" Harry asked.

"Most had no match on the database," she said. "Apart from Marsh, the only other positive match was a man called Callum McBain."

Harry turned pale. His breath caught in his throat. Had he heard right? "Sorry? Who?"

"Callum McBain," Hettie repeated.

He felt as if he'd been punched in the guts. His demons were back, risen up from the place he'd banished them to. Callum McBain belonged to Harry's past. He was a vicious killer Harry wanted to forget.

"He's not local," Hettie continued. "I took the liberty of looking him up on the database. He was a villain from Glasgow, the police up there believe him to be dead. He was part of a large organised crime operation up in Scotland."

But Harry wasn't listening. The name Callum McBain was still ringing in his ears. It had tripped off Hettie's tongue so easily, as if it meant nothing at all, but it had left Harry gasping for air. He'd not heard that name or that of anyone connected with that world in a long while, and he was totally unprepared to hear it now. Why hadn't Sandy warned him? If McBain was dead, that meant only one thing. He'd crossed his arch rival once too often. But what was the connection with the case here in Ryebridge? Did it mean the man who haunted Harry's nightmares had found him? Was this a warning? He felt sick.

Harry couldn't think straight. He was floored. No way could he hang around and wait to hear who else Hettie might dredge up. He needed to be outside and alone. Leaving the others gaping, Harry dashed off through the main doors.

Outside, he threw up. Had Mungo Salton found him? It wouldn't be difficult, he had enough contacts. Was he on his patch right now, orchestrating events? Had he killed Sutton and Marsh to taunt him? Finding bits of McBain on the hand was possibly no accident. The last thing Harry needed was the past dragging up. The horror of what had happened three years ago was enough to live with without having it thrust down his throat by people mentioning familiar names — or worse, seeing familiar faces.

Wasn't it punishment enough that he had to carry the memory of it with him, seared into his mind's eye? It never left him, the image of that building engulfed in flames. He could even smell the smoke. Worst of all were his brother's screams. He could hear them too, they followed him everywhere. Harry looked down at his scarred hands and began to weep. Why hadn't he been able to save him? Why?

* * *

"What happened to you?" Jess asked when he returned ten minutes later, still pale.

"Sorry about that. Dodgy sausage at breakfast I reckon." He caught sight of Jess winking at Hettie. They'd obviously been talking about him.

"I'll compile the report and put it on the system," Hettie said.

Jess grabbed his arm. "C'mon, let's get you some water and summat for that stomach."

"I'm fine, honest. Just got caught short, that's all."

"I had the sausages too and I'm fine," she said.

"I got unlucky. It happens."

* * *

They were back at the car, with Jess at the wheel. "Want to talk? There's obviously something going on with you. That name,

Callum McBain, you recognised it, didn't you? Don't lie to me. Who is he?"

"You're wrong, I've never heard of him. I was about to throw up my breakfast and needed to get outside. No mystery, Jess."

But Jess believed different. This was typical of Harry. He knew the name all right, and she guessed he knew the man too. But she couldn't help him if he refused to confide in her.

"What now? Back to the station? Find out more about McBain?" she said.

Harry had no choice. Much as he wanted to forget all about the man, they had to deal with the evidence Hettie had uncovered. "You do that. I'll look into Lancashire Holdings."

"What's the betting they're connected? Have to be. The man who did that to McBain did the same to Nick and Andy. It'll be him, whoever he is, that bought the factory, I'll lay money on it. D'you have any names to offer up?"

God, he hoped she wasn't right, but the evidence was there.

"Go on, names, you must have some idea."

Only one and it was raging through his head. But no way could Harry say it, not yet. "We can't be certain of anything until we find the bodies," he said, looking away.

"You think they're definitely dead then?"

"Oh yes. If McBain's people are involved, there's no doubt about it. As for McBain himself, he must have crossed the boss to end up like Sutton and Marsh."

"See! I knew you were familiar with the name. Why don't you just come clean, Harry? We can't go on tiptoeing around this — or each other. We've a case to solve, we're getting nowhere and meanwhile you clam up on me."

Jess was annoyed. She'd had enough of Harry's secrecy. One way or another she would find out what he was hiding. He knew it too, so why not just tell her?

"Another time, Jess, promise. But I'm not up to discussing McBain right now."

"His cohorts, or enemies then. D'you know who they are? Do you have any clue at all about who is behind this?"

"Possibly, but I hope to God I'm wrong. The man I have in mind is toxic and if this is down to him, we're really in trouble."

CHAPTER TWENTY-THREE

When they got back to the office, Harry muttered something about needing air and went off for a walk round the town to clear his head. Jess took advantage of his absence to contact the Glasgow force and ask about Callum McBain. The man she spoke to, a DI Gregor Laing, was only too willing to help. He had such a strong Glaswegian accent that she had trouble understanding him. The DI remembered Harry Lennox very well.

"He was my DS for a while, a few years ago now," he said. "Pleasant young man, tipped to go far, but that case really messed with his life. I suppose he's told you all about it."

"A little," she lied, "It was a shame what happened." If she admitted to this man that Harry hadn't told her anything, he might wonder why.

"A shame? What happened was a bloody tragedy. I'm not surprised he had to get away. Anyway, why are you asking about McBain now?" he said.

"His name has come up in one of our enquiries," Jess told him. "We believe he's been murdered by an unknown killer we're looking for."

"Harry know?"

"Yes, and I don't think he's taking it well. He threw up when McBain was mentioned."

"I'm not surprised. That was some experience and it must have left its mark. Give him my best, will you? He's a good lad. I hope what happened didn't damage his life too much."

Interesting, but it didn't tell her much. Jess was tempted to ask more but thought it might reveal her ignorance of what happened. "We think someone known to him has bought a local clothing manufacturing business, but we have no idea why."

"McBain and the people he mixed with were into drugs, girls, money-laundering and various other scams, but never clothing." He paused. "Surely Harry has told you about McBain, about the gangs and the rivalry"

How to answer that one! Jess finally decided the truth was best. "No. I was hoping you could help me."

Another pause. "Harry's not said anything at all, has he? I'd say ask him, but I can imagine the reaction you'd get."

"Could you give me a name, or any other information that will help us?"

"I'll give you a name, but you do not repeat it to Harry, understood? He has to be the one to bring it up. Do you agree?"

"Yes."

"Mungo Salton," he almost whispered. "Callum McBain ran a gang in Glasgow. His biggest rival was Salton. The pair kept the force on their toes, I can tell you. With McBain dead that leaves Salton with the patch all to himself. That is some opportunity and he's sure to make the most of it. The problem we have is that currently he's nowhere to be found. Word round here is that Salton has taken off, but we don't know where. He could surface anywhere, anytime. This enquiry of yours, that's how you know McBain is dead?"

"Yes."

"Then I'd say you have a problem. Let's hope Salton doesn't surface near you, for Harry's sake."

"Why haven't you got the man locked up if he's so dangerous?"

"He's tricky, knows the law. Whenever a case against him gets to court, he hires the best, pays people off and makes it all go away. I'm sure you know villains like that. We've even had him banged up, but he's a model prisoner. As far as we know, he's not put a foot wrong since he was last released. He may be your man. I just hope I'm wrong because Harry couldn't take crossing swords with him again."

"Thanks. That gives me some background," Jess said.

"A word of warning, hen. If Salton is active again and on your patch, don't let Harry get near him. Dangerous doesn't cover it — the man's an animal. He won't think twice about putting a bullet in his head."

"And knowing that, you still haven't been able to put him behind bars?" Jess said.

"So far we've only got him on minor stuff, and he's done months or a couple of years. We know he's killed folk, but the proof has always eluded us. He's evil, bad to the core and Harry hates him, so watch he doesn't take risks. He'll be tempted to have a go after what happened to his brother."

His brother? This was news. Harry had never mentioned any brother. In the two years she'd worked with him, he hadn't said a word.

"I didn't know about him," she said. She was hoping the admission would lead DI Laing to tell her more, but it simply angered him.

"He really hasn't told you anything, has he? You're pumping me for information because Harry won't tell you. It won't work, hen, not with me. Harry obviously has his reasons for keeping what happened out of his new life and I've got to respect that."

"Sorry. It was stupid of me. But I'm genuinely worried about him, and that's why I called you. This is affecting his work, and you've no idea how he's living or how much he drinks. Now I'm beginning to see why. He's got a past and is trying hard to bury it, but it isn't working. It's just making him ill."

"You could be right, but my advice is to leave it be. If Harry wants to talk, he will."

"Okay. I just hope that one of these days he might trust me enough to tell me what happened before he crumbles completely. Thanks for your help."

"I didn't mean to bite your head off, lass. But Harry is a complicated person. He might appear all bluff good humour but that's just an act to cover his real emotions. Believe me, the real Harry is quite different. And don't forget to give him my best."

Jess immediately turned to her computer, eager to do some research, look up Harry's brother's birth record for one, and find out what had become of him. Was he injured? Dead! And what did his fate have to do with McBain or Salton? But her questions remained unanswered. She got a call on the office phone from the desk sergeant. Jess could tell immediately that something had happened.

"The bodies of two men have been found," he said. "The PC that stumbled on them suspects it's Sutton and Marsh, although no formal identification has been done yet. I'll give you the location."

"Local?"

"Yes. D'you know the lorry park at the back of Shaw's Haulage?"

"I know it. Were they left in the open?"

"No, they were in a container." he sighed. "Happy days, eh. I'll get the SOCOs on it."

Jess had to find Harry, he should know at once. She put the notes from her conversation with DI Laing in her bag. She'd continue her research at home.

CHAPTER TWENTY-FOUR

McBain's name and the memories it dredged up had put Harry in a foul mood. He strode unseeing around town and ended up in the park. He was sitting on a bench, thinking about the past when Jess's call jolted him back to the present and his wretched life. She was right, he couldn't continue like this. He'd have to deal with the past, face up to it, demons and all.

Harry didn't say a word on their way to the haulage yard. Only when they had arrived and were making their way towards the group of white-suited SOCOs did he speak. "Do most of these vehicles and containers belong to Shaw's Haulage?"

"I've no idea. I know as much as you do about the firm."

"Yes, but you've lived round here all your life. I presumed you'd know these things," he said abruptly.

"Don't take your bad mood out on me, Harry Lennox. We all have off days, but we don't bring our moods to work with us. It's called growing up."

"I'm the senior officer here, remember. I think you forget that far too often."

Jess strode out in front of him. "Well, sir, stuff you!"

Now he'd done it. He hadn't meant to upset her. It was just that she happened to be the person nearest to him, so she always ended up as the butt of his bad moods. He constantly vented his frustration on poor Jess because he couldn't deal with what was really bothering him.

He quickened his pace and caught up with her. "I'm sorry, I'm an idiot. It's personal stuff that's making me tetchy. It's not your fault."

"Too damn right it's not," she retorted. "You've got some nerve behaving the way you do. Why not just get whatever's bothering you off your chest and then I can try to help."

"You can't help me, Jess, no one can."

She strode off again. "Have it your own way."

"This place," he shouted after her. "Sure you know nothing about it?"

"I think it's used by a few haulage firms." She pointed to the signage on one or two of the doors. "But Shaw's own the plot."

"Are we okay?" he asked. "I didn't intend to upset you, really. I just need to calm down."

"Where did you get to? I rang your mobile several times but you didn't pick up for ages."

"Sorry, I went for a walk. I was trying to make sense of what we're up against."

"And did you?" she asked. "Clear your mind? Make sense of it all?"

"No. The personal stuff got in the way, so I'm still confused about the case. I'm hoping the forensics from this little lot will help."

"That personal stuff must be a biggy. But if you insist on keeping it all bottled up, there's not a lot I can do."

Melanie Trent greeted them at the container doors. She didn't look happy. "Whoever did this has done an excellent clean up job. The inside reeks of bleach, it's so strong you can hardly breathe. They didn't bother with the bodies though. I suspect they've been hosed down, but that's it."

"Is it them?" Jess asked.

Melanie handed them each a paper coverall from a pile beside her. "Get into these and see for yourselves. It's not pretty. Both of them have been badly beaten, particularly about the face and head."

"Who found them?" Harry asked.

"That driver over there. The container doors were blowing in the wind, so he came over to close them. Got one helluva shock."

"Any attempt made to hide their identities?" Harry asked.

"Doesn't look like it. Both are missing a left hand, but we can easily get prints from the right ones."

"Are you up for this?" Harry asked Jess. "This is the least pleasant part of the job, and despite how you act, I know you're no toughie."

"I've seen a few dead bodies in my time," she said. "Don't worry about me. It's you that's got the dodgy guts and all the personal baggage, remember."

Melanie Trent hadn't been joking when she said it wasn't pretty. It was one of the most harrowing murder scenes either detective had ever witnessed. The two men were naked, suspended by their right arms from a bar fixed into the roof of the container.

"Both have what at first sight appears to be a dislocated right shoulder joint, which makes me think they were hanging like that for some time while still alive. Must have hurt like hell." Melanie grimaced. "I'll know the extent of the damage and attempt an estimate of how long they were kept like that back at the morgue."

"There are burn marks on the container wall here," Hettie said. "They've had a good go at cleaning, but they obviously couldn't get the marks off."

"An attempt to prevent them from bleeding to death. This wasn't just about killing this pair. Was it about punishment or did the killers want something from them, but what? Take the hands and cauterise the wounds, keep them going for a bit longer," Harry said. "So, they must have used something for that. Any idea what?"

"A blow torch perhaps," Melanie said. "Again, we'll see what traces we find back at the lab."

Harry took a closer look at the body of Nick Sutton. The stump from where his hand had been severed had definitely been burned, but it hadn't been particularly well done, and it had still bled afterwards. Both men had extensive bruising over most of their bodies.

"Sutton was hit about the head with something hard. He'd have been out of it for some time. Marsh, on the other hand, only has superficial bruises on his face and head. But his body has been badly beaten. I'd say with a clublike instrument — a baseball bat would do it. What killed them both was gunshot wounds to the head. Both were shot at close range through the mouth, pointing upwards. A shotgun I'd say. There are large exit wounds at the top of their heads."

"Any bullets?" asked Harry.

"Yes, we found these." Hettie showed Harry an evidence bag containing some spent cartridges. "No attempt was made to hide them, they were left lying on the floor. Which is odd given how careful they've been about everything else."

"Any chance of prints or DNA?" asked Jess.

"The whole place has been sluiced down, and liberal amounts of bleach were used. I doubt we'll get anything useful."

"Do Shaw's have an office nearby?" Harry asked Jess.

"There's a building at the back of that fence. We could try there."

"We need a word with the owner. I want to know all about this container, who it belongs to and who used it last."

CHAPTER TWENTY-FIVE

Roger Shaw ran the haulage firm with his father. Given what had happened, the office was closed for the day. But Shaw had been alerted by the police and was waiting for them.

"The business was started by my dad, but he's more or less retired now," he explained. "He only comes in a couple of times a month. I see to our own day-to-day work, and I also rent out space to other firms to park up their vehicles overnight or at weekends." He checked his records. "That particular container came in four days ago from Glasgow. The lorry that transported it is registered to Lancashire Holdings, not a company I'm familiar with. Does that help? I see from the booking that it was one my father dealt with. Is there a problem with it?"

"A problem? Do you have any idea what happened out there?" Harry said angrily. "Two people have been murdered in the most horrific way. They must have screamed, begged for their lives. Didn't your staff hear anything?"

"There's not many of us here during the weekend, just Saturday morning perhaps. We tend to confine what we do to weekdays, Mr Lennox. That way we get less hassle from the neighbours. The wall you see at the back is all that separates us from the Baxendale estate, and they complain like hell about the noise."

"Have Lancashire Holdings parked their containers here before?"

"Not that I can see from the records. They'll be a relatively small enterprise. The firms who use our overnight parking facility tend to be privately owned — one lorry, one container types. As for Lancashire Holdings, I've no idea, I'm afraid."

"Can we speak to your father, see if he recalls anything about the booking?" Harry asked.

"He's not well so I left him at home. My dad has memory problems, I'm afraid. He might recall something useful, then again, he may have no idea what you're talking about. What I can tell you is that the booking was made over the phone and paid for by a debit card in the name of Lancashire Holdings."

Harry handed him a card. "If your dad remembers anything, could you write it down for us? And anyone else contacts you from Lancashire Holdings, ring us at once."

"Can we reopen now?"

"Once the forensic team have finished. Do you have many employees, Mr Shaw?"

"Me or my dad in the office, and half a dozen drivers. They haven't been here since Thursday. All six are on the continent, due back tomorrow."

"Chose their moment well," Jess said once they were outside.

"Did their research more like," Harry replied. "Back to the station, and let's get on with some research of our own. We need to know a lot more about Lancashire Holdings, where their office is will do for starters."

"Interesting that the lorry and container came from Glasgow. It goes with finding bits of Callum McBain on Nick Sutton's hand, doesn't it?"

Harry winced, whether at the image in his head or the sound of that name he wasn't sure. Maybe both. "I doubt the Glasgow angle will come to much."

"We don't know that. It certainly merits investigating."

* * *

With both detectives on the job, it didn't take long to find out something about Lancashire Holdings. Jess discovered that the business had only been operational for three months, too soon to file any returns. The company's registered office was in Preston. Scanning the record, she saw there was only one director listed.

"Harry," she called. "Lancashire Holdings. I have a director's name."

Harry held his breath, believing he already knew. It had to be him. Who else could it be? He waited for Jess to pronounce the name that haunted his nightmares, it twisted his guts just to think about it. He clenched his fists under the desk and braced himself.

"Guess what," she called. "Their one and only director is none other than our own Ryan Cassidy."

Harry breathed out. Who would have believed it? Instantly, his mood lightened. But did Ryan have the ability to set something like this up? He couldn't see it somehow. Harry smiled to himself. Anyway, he could stop worrying and get his head back in gear, press on with the job.

He tapped a pen on the desk, in thinking mode. "Let's look at what we've got, Jessie. Two bodies, done to death in a horrific way. Lethal drugs sold on the Baxendale and skirmishes among the gangs."

"Don't forget the takeovers, possibly by Ryan Cassidy — Sutton's factory and those rented properties," Jess said. "We'll have to bring him in."

"I don't see this being down to Ryan, the lad hasn't got the brains for it. But we'll bring him in anyway, see how he reacts to what we've got," Harry said.

"I'm doing a little research and I've come up with something interesting. The lethal drugs were sold to people living in three of the houses belonging to Sutton. Someone clearing the way, I wonder?" Jess said.

"What for?" Harry asked.

"I don't know," she said, "but wouldn't you say that someone wants those houses? Kill off the occupants and that becomes much easier. And don't forget, Ryan Cassidy knows the area and the people living in those houses very well. What about the other two that Sutton owned?"

"One is a known drugs den," he said, "officially empty but in fact it's used as a place to doss down for the night, and the other was officially empty but is likely being used by the homeless. It might be useful to know if anyone dossing down in those two houses has been threatened, told to leave. Perhaps they could give us a description."

"Everyone round here knows the Cassidys, so no need. The problem is, will they be prepared to shop them to us?" Jean said.

Harry nodded but he wasn't really listening. He'd had an idea. "That oil found on Sutton's hand, it could have come from a lorry. The rough ground of that parking area was covered in the stuff, that and diesel."

"You're right," Jess said. "We should get Hettie to run more tests."

"Meanwhile, we need to pay that visit to Ryan."

"I'll get my jacket," Jess said.

As they were leaving, a uniformed PC stopped them on the stairs. "We've got a problem, sir. There's a riot cracking off on the Baxendale. It looks like it's centred on a house near to where Kelsey Green lived."

Jess checked the addresses they had for the Sutton properties and showed him. "Is it one of those?"

"Yes, number seventeen, the one being used as a drugs den, and it's looking as if it's starting to get nasty."

Harry looked at Jess. "What d'you reckon? Irate users and no supply?"

"If we don't step in, sir, someone could get killed," the PC said.

"Do we know who is responsible?" Harry asked.

"The new landlords want them out, a firm called Lancashire Holdings. They have people there now, breaking down the door and frightening the natives to death."

Harry looked at Jess. "Busy bunch, this firm, aren't they? Okay, Constable, we'll assemble a team and get round there."

CHAPTER TWENTY-SIX

The PC hadn't been joking when he called it a riot. The problem was, the rioters were the neighbouring residents. It turned out that bailiffs were the ones doing the evictions at the house, so it was all legal and above board. Whoever they found currently living in or using number seventeen had to leave today. The original tenants had long since gone but notice of the repossession had been sent to the property, purporting to be because of unpaid rent.

"How long before it's us they're throwing onto the streets?" a man yelled at them. "I don't like that lazy lot any better than you, but we'll be next. Bloody company wants the whole estate."

Harry spoke to one of the PCs. "Have a word with him. Find out exactly what he means and if he's been approached by anyone."

Several dishevelled-looking blokes were standing about on the pavement holding sleeping bags and duvets. Harry presumed these were the homeless who'd just been turfed out. One was screaming at the bailiffs and throwing stones. But there were still others inside, and they were refusing to leave.

"They've nowhere to go," Jess said. "Dossing down in that hole is obviously preferable to a night on the streets, particularly when it's pouring with rain."

"We can't fix everything, Jessie," Harry said. "They'll have to take pot luck with the council." He pointed to a young man with a haversack on his back, dressed in weatherproof jacket and trousers. "He doesn't look like he belongs. Think I'll have a word. I don't recognise him, do you?"

"Not one of the regulars," she said. "Perhaps he's new to the area."

Harry went across to the young man. "Sorry stuff, but the bailiffs have the law on their side. You got somewhere to go?"

"Yep. I'll doss down at a mate's. Shame, I was hoping to hang around for a few nights."

"These houses have been bought. No doubt they'll be done up and sold off at a huge profit," Jess said, joining them. "Has anyone from the new owners ever visited?"

"Not that I'm aware of. All I know is that several houses around here have been bought by some firm and they don't want us hanging around," the young man said.

"Was that company called Lancashire Holdings by any chance?" she asked him.

"No idea. Look, all I did was bed down here a couple of nights. It was never my intention to hang around."

Harry was looking at the repossession paperwork that he'd got from the bailiffs. It bothered him that three residents of the five houses once owned by Sutton were dead, Kelsey Green being one of them.

"We know about the dealing that goes on round here. We don't like it, but until recently it hadn't killed anyone. Did you know Kelsey?" he asked the young man. "She lived over there."

"Kept myself to myself, safest way I find. Look, I'll have to go if I'm to make it to my mate's tonight. Hope you get it sorted."

Jess and Harry watched him walk away. "He definitely doesn't fit in round here. Wrong accent for a start," Jess said. "Bet you're relieved it's not Scottish. More Europe somewhere, I'd say."

Their conversation was cut short by one of the Cassidy boys — Caleb, the youngest. He had been trying to protect one of his mates, who was staggering out through the doorway of number seventeen obviously off his head on something. "They've no right, messing with the area like this," Caleb said angrily. "I've a good mind to sort a couple of them. Let 'em know they can't push us around."

"Keep out of it," Harry said. "Get lippy or use those fists of yours and you'll end up at the station."

"You're better off going home," Jess shouted to him above the clamour. "This is getting nasty and any minute now, the police will be making arrests."

Harry had his hands over his ears. The screaming and shouting had got louder, but it was the sound of fireworks going off nearby that was doing his head in.

Caleb Cassidy was about to dive back into the fray when Jess grabbed hold of his hoodie. "You know folk around here. What about the lad we were just talking to a few minutes ago?"

"Zeno? He's harmless but he does know the dude who's been dealing that wrong stuff. Giving it away for the most part."

"You mean the stuff that killed Kelsey?" Caleb nodded. "Are you sure about that, Caleb? Do you have any proof?"

Harry darted off after Zeno. Find him and he could help, but the streetlights were out and it was pitch black. There was no way he could catch him now. He might have gone anywhere.

"His mate gave me some of those little packets he was dishing out," Caleb told Jess. "But I didn't take any. My mum would have had a fit if I'd gone home drugged up."

"What did you do with them?" Harry asked, having failed to catch up with the Zeno character.

110

Caleb Cassidy stuck his hands in his jacket pockets and pulled out about ten small plastic bags. "Here, you 'ave 'em. They're no use to me."

Harry put them in an evidence bag. He'd get Hettie to check if it was the same mix that had killed Kelsey.

"D'you know who made this stuff?" Harry asked him.

"Foreign bloke, big brute of a man. He dossed down in one of the houses for a while, but I think he's shacked up somewhere else now."

"Zeno, you said. Odd name. D'you know what his mate was called, Caleb?" Jess asked.

The lad was edgy, reluctant to say more. "Look, I've got to get back in there, my mate's in a bad way. He's got a beat-up leg and can hardly walk."

"You promise to come down to the station tomorrow and we'll get you and your mate a lift home. I want you to tell us everything you know about that Zeno person and the man who gave the drugs to Kelsey."

Caleb nodded. "All right. But I don't know much. He just turned up one day and started dishing out the dope like it were sweets. Didn't want no money either."

"Okay, Caleb, you're off the hook for now. But if you remember anything else about him, you contact me," Jess told him. "When you've got your mate, the PC over there will take you home."

"We should bring in Ryan before it gets too late. They planned to go away, remember," Harry said. "We'll get round there, take him down to the station. He can answer our questions under caution."

* * *

Harry and Jess left the police and bailiffs to it. Once they were in the relative quiet of the car, Harry rang the station and alerted them to the lad Zeno. He gave a brief description and instructed uniform to bring him in if he was spotted. They drove away.

"I wouldn't have thought Ryan Cassidy had the brains to put together a complex operation like this. If it is him, he's managed to rid the area of two villains, taken over their property and who knows what else."

"Ryan is the only director of Lancashire Holdings," Jess said. "It's all there, in the public domain for anyone to see."

"I'll interview him with a PC. Meanwhile, I want you to find out about that Zeno bloke. Search the system, see if you can find a likely candidate. There can't be many villains with that name."

"Harry, you do realise that if Ryan is involved then he must know Zeno and his mate. They could have cleared the way. D'you think it's possible that they did all the dirty stuff and Ryan is the acceptable face?"

"But we don't know that Ryan had anything to do with the killings," Harry said.

"For his sake, I hope that's how it is."

CHAPTER TWENTY-SEVEN

Ryan Cassidy was not happy about being dragged down to the station. "You know me and Adele are about to fly off. I miss that plane and she'll bloody kill me."

"You've got some explaining to do first, Ryan. For starters, you can tell me about Lancashire Holdings."

Harry sat back and watched Ryan's reaction. The young man was either genuinely puzzled or a bloody good actor. He certainly didn't look like someone who'd just been found out.

Ryan looked round at the solicitor, who was making notes. "What's he on about?" he asked. "I've never heard of these holdings. This is all new to me, Copper."

"Ryan, you know what Companies House is?" Harry asked.

Ryan nodded. "Yeah. It's for when you get limited and the like."

"They list all the companies in the UK, along with the names of their directors. Lancashire Holdings is cited as having one director — you, Ryan." Harry paused, waiting for a reaction.

"Sorry, mate, but I don't understand. I've never heard of them," Ryan said.

"Which is a shame because I was hoping you could tell me what their business is, and how many people they employ."

"Are you off your 'ead or what? I'm not a director of anything. True, me and Adele have thought about starting something of our own. I've spoken to Craig Sutton about buying into his car showroom business, but that's it."

"The family car repair business not good enough for you?" Harry asked.

"I've wanted out since the day I first set foot in that workshop at sixteen," Ryan said. "Problem is, cars are all I know, though according to Craig, I don't look half bad in a suit." He grinned. "My ma works us into the ground. She never lets up. If I don't get out, I'll go mad."

"So, you set up Lancashire Holdings?"

"No," Ryan said. "I've told you. I don't know anything about that. I'm a practical type, I fix stuff, I'm good with my hands. I don't know owt about setting up no limited company."

Seeing Ryan's obvious confusion, Harry believed him. Ryan had probably been set up. He was the perfect target, from the perfect family — all well-known troublemakers from the Baxendale.

"We'll have to investigate more, but if we find no evidence that you're involved, you'll be off the hook," Harry said.

Heaving a sigh of relief, Ryan made to stand up.

Harry held up his hand. "Not so fast. What d'you know about the drug dealing on the Baxendale and the houses being bought up?"

"It's not down to me, if that's what you're getting at," Ryan said indignantly.

Harry leaned back and folded his arms. "We know it's down to Lancashire Holdings and possibly a mate of a young man called Zeno. Know him?"

"Look, I know nothing about drugs, and as for the houses, the last places I'd want to buy was ones on that rundown hellhole. You'd be better off asking our Caleb, he hangs out down the Baxendale. He knows the dealers, the regulars I mean. I did hear that there's been someone new recently. That might be this Zeno you're on about. Caleb didn't trust him. Said he was right dodgy, far too nicely dressed for a dealer."

Harry nodded. Maybe he could tease more out of Ryan before he let him go. "He told me about Zeno. Have you met him?"

"No. Since I left ma's I don't get to the Baxendale. Adele don't like the place."

"Has Caleb ever rung him? Met up with him, perhaps in a special place?"

"I doubt it. Caleb's not into owt like that."

"Someone is, and everywhere I turn your name pops up, Ryan. I don't want to believe you're involved, so that means someone out there thinks you're easy to frame. Any ideas?"

"No. Look, I just want to go home."

"I'm investigating two murders and three overdoses that are down to someone on the Baxendale giving them cocaine cut with fentanyl. Know anything about that?" Harry said.

"No. I'm not a druggie and I don't mix with any. You know what that place is. It could be down to anyone, but it has nothing to do with me." Ryan glanced up at the clock. "Can I go home now?"

It was late. Harry wouldn't mind getting off himself, and he could murder a beer. "Okay. But you surrender your passport. I don't want you leaving the country until this little lot is sorted. The PC here will give you a lift home and you'll hand it over to him. Got it?"

"So, no holiday?"

"No, tell Adele she'll have to wait." A sudden thought occurred to Harry. "The money. A win on the horses Adele said. Which bookies?"

Ryan leaned forward and put his head in his hands. "You'll find out anyway, I suppose. I didn't win that money. It was left on my doorstep a week ago."

"How much?"

"Ten grand."

"And you didn't wonder where it had come from?" Harry said.

Ryan brought his head up sharply. "No, I bloody didn't! It was just the boost me and Adele needed. I stuck it in the bank, no questions asked."

Harry studied the young man. "Was there a note with the money?"

"No, and it was in mixed used notes in an old brown envelope."

"D'you still have it, the envelope I mean?"

"Adele stuck it in the bin."

"Right, Ryan. This is what's going to happen. A PC will take you home, and a forensic team will salvage that envelope. How often is the bin emptied?"

"It's the paper and cardboard one, so not until next week."

"You can't keep that money either. It's the proceeds of a crime and will have to be confiscated," Harry said.

CHAPTER TWENTY-EIGHT

Day Six

Harry put his hands to his ears and groaned. It was early, barely light, but the din was loud enough to wake the dead. Someone was banging on the camper van door so hard they were in danger of punching a hole through it.

"Laddie, let me in!"

At the sound of the familiar voice, Harry's eyes opened wide. For a moment, he wondered if he was dreaming, but a crafty peek through the blinds confirmed that Sandy was real. His immediate reaction was panic. He had a desperate urge to hide. What was Sandy doing here? And why hadn't he phoned first? Harry was totally unprepared for this. Where would he put him for starters, and what to tell his old friend about his current situation?

More banging and shouting. Sandy wasn't about to give up. Grabbing his dressing gown, Harry got out of bed and yanked open the door.

"You took your time," Sandy said. "Let an old man in out of the cold, would ye, and get me a hot drink."

"Sandy, you should have said you were coming, I'd have . . ."

Sandy Munro looked around him. "What? Had a go at cleaning this midden?"

"It's not that bad," Harry said feebly.

"It's a mess, and so are you from what I hear."

Harry could do without this right now. "What d'you mean? Who's been telling tales?"

"That young woman, your sergeant, had a word with Laing. Wanted to know about you and your work in Glasgow. I reckon he told her more than he should have. Mentioned our mutual friend, not that she recognised the name, and that started the tittle-tattle again. People at your old station are still asking the same old questions and coming up with the same old theories."

Harry sat down hard on the bed. Why couldn't his past stay that way — in the past, safely back in Glasgow? Folk back home could gossip all they wanted but Jess was another matter. He didn't want her knowing about Salton. That would really open the floodgates. She'd never let up. Jess would want to know things about him he wasn't ready to share. "She hasn't mentioned it. Mind you, we've been a bit busy."

"Am I getting that tea or what?"

Harry scratched his head. "Give me ten to get cleaned up and dressed and I'll take you for breakfast. Have you got somewhere to stay?"

"I was hoping that you might give me a bed for a couple of nights, but there's no way I'd sleep in this — sorry, lad."

"Don't worry, we'll find you somewhere."

* * *

Harry could have killed Jess. Why did she have to stick her nose in? The last thing he wanted was Sandy under his feet. Once he was in Don's house, out of earshot and heading for the shower, he rang her.

"You've given me one huge problem," he said angrily. "Your little heart-to-heart with Greg Laing has resulted in a visit from Sandy."

"What's wrong with that? You should be pleased. He's an old friend, after all. Now you can have that catch-up."

"Don't try being flippant with me, Jess, it's no joke. Sandy belongs back home, on his own patch, far away from mine."

"Why, Harry? Why won't you let anyone from your past into your present life? What are you hiding? All this secrecy is beginning to piss me off. We've worked together for two years and I can count the things I know about you on the fingers of one hand."

"I'm really not that interesting, so butt out."

He finished the call. Jess had no right to interfere like this. He'd just finished dressing and was on his way back to join Sandy when there was a call from a PC who was helping with the Lucy Green case.

"DI Maxwell asked me to ring you," he said. "He's found out something regarding the shoes that were found on the path. Turns out they were bought from Allen's in town but had to be ordered because they didn't have the right colour in stock. The order specified the correct size so the kid must have been measured for them sometime before she disappeared. They were paid for in cash."

"Do we know who bought them?"

"This is why DI Maxwell said I should update you, sir. He knows you're off the case, but the person who ordered and paid for the shoes was a young woman. The way the owner described her I thought it sounded like Kelsey Green, the mother. What makes this interesting is the date, it was after Lucy went missing."

If Kelsey ordered those shoes, it meant she knew where Lucy was. Otherwise, why order them? So why pretend she'd been taken? Harry would have a word with the staff at Allen's himself, show them a photo of Kelsey and see if they recognised her.

CHAPTER TWENTY-NINE

"I've got to go to work, Sandy," Harry told his friend when he returned. He saw his friend's face fall and immediately felt guilty. *It'll be okay*, he told himself. But apprehension was making him edgy. The last thing Harry wanted was his past shoving in his face.

"What, no chat? No breakfast? But, laddie, you promised."

Fair comment. He owed him that much. Sandy had come a long way. All Harry wanted was to get him out of the way, but the least he could do was feed him first. "Okay, but it'll have to be quick."

"Off to the station then?"

"No, a newsagents' about five miles away. I'm knee deep in a murder case, Sandy. I really don't have a lot of time for socialising."

"You don't have to worry about me, I can amuse myself. That sergeant of yours, is she going with you?"

"No, I'll ring her in a bit. She can get on with something else." A thought suddenly occurred to Harry. "If you do bump into her and she asks, you're an old friend of the family. All right? When you rang the other day, you caught me on the hop. Jess was curious. If I'd told her anything else, there'd have been questions, hence the lie."

"I'm honoured, but why not just tell her the truth, that I'm your old boss and proud of it? We worked well together, we were a good team, until . . ."

Harry gave the older man a quizzical look. "You sure about the team thing? Because if I was you, I'd be wondering about that."

"Oh, I've got questions, and some theories, but another time. Later perhaps, over a pint."

That tone. Harry knew it of old. There was unfinished business between them. The ageing DCI was evidently happy to play the long game.

"Look, I've no problem with you being here, but I just ask one thing. If you spend any time with Jess, my sergeant, don't bring up the past or anything to do with my work in Glasgow. She will ask, she's nosy, that's what makes her such a good detective."

"Okay, I'll keep it light. Point me in the direction of a reasonable bed and breakfast and I'll be fine. Perhaps some food first though, and then I'll have a wander around the town until you get back from work. Tonight, we'll go to your local and have that talk."

Harry nodded. He didn't relish the prospect. He knew where 'that talk' might lead. And Sandy with a drink inside him could be trouble.

* * *

At the café in the shopping mall, Harry got a coffee to go and left Sandy tucking into the works and chatting happily with Elsie. Harry knew he should take Jess with him, but he couldn't face the interrogation. He rang and left her a message. He wanted the mobile records for Ryan Cassidy, Nick Sutton, and Andy Marsh. Urgently. He'd look at them later. He also wanted to ensure that the brown paper envelope had reached the Reid okay. The more he thought about it, the more he believed that someone was using Ryan Cassidy, pointing them in his direction as a smokescreen, albeit a temporary one.

First thing on his list was the shoe shop. He had to know for sure who it was that collected the pair ordered for Lucy. Fortunately for Harry, the owner of Allen's Shoes, one Irfan Hussain, remembered the woman who had picked them up.

Harry showed Irfan Kelsey's photo on his mobile. "Is this her?"

Irfan took the mobile and studied the image. "Ah yes. That is the woman. Very loud she was. We had to search for the package in the back and she became very agitated, said she had somewhere to be. I remember her because she was pretty rude, actually. Swore at me."

"And she paid cash?"

"Yes. I recall it because she had a bundle of fifty pound notes in her purse. Something else, I had the feeling she didn't want to be seen," Irfan said. "She acted as if she was hiding her face from that camera up there."

"What date was this?"

"Exactly two weeks ago. I remember because it was the same day as my wife's birthday."

"Has she been back since?" Harry asked.

"No, she's not a regular."

Harry went back to his car. There was no doubt, Kelsey had collected the shoes weeks after Lucy's disappearance. There was no logical reason for that other than she'd known very well that her daughter was alive and well. What he couldn't understand was why Kelsey had staged her own daughter's disappearance. Why would she do that? Money, he supposed. This case posed mystery after mystery and it was doing Harry's head in.

CHAPTER THIRTY

"Get anything?" Jess asked.

Harry had just come into the main office. "More stuff that doesn't add up," he said. "You?"

"All three of them — Sutton, Marsh and Cassidy — made and received calls from pay-as-you-go mobiles with no contact attached to them. In each case no more than twice, and it was a different mobile number for each of them," Jess said.

"A different number for each call — security gone wild. Wonder why?"

"If it was the same caller, they were probably trying to confuse us. Marsh and Sutton both used their personal mobiles the evening they were last seen, Marsh made a call to Babs, and Sutton to Caroline."

That made sense. "About earlier," he said. "Sorry if I was a bit off."

"A bit! You were bloody awful, and for no reason either. I've done you a favour. You could do with seeing someone from home, it'll do you good."

Harry doubted that. Having to deal with Sandy over the next day or so would be like negotiating a complex game of chess. And he'd likely be the loser.

"We'll have to speak to Martha again," he said soberly. "I think someone's trying to ensure Martha's lot are in the frame for as much as possible. I just don't know why, other than they are well known troublemakers."

"We'll have that word and while we're at it, see what she has to say about Lancashire Holdings," Jess said.

But Harry shook his head. "I don't think we should do that."

"Why not? How many reasons do you need? Ryan is named as a director of that company. Martha might be an innocent party, but she could also be complicit. We need to interview her properly, Harry. Find out what she knows."

Jess was studying Harry's notes. "The Cassidys are a rough bunch, they steal things and are ready to use their fists instead of talking stuff through. Perhaps whoever is orchestrating this wants rid of them every bit as much as they wanted rid of Sutton and Marsh. Whatever is planned for that factory and those houses, they don't want any interference from Martha and her clan," Jess suggested.

"Yes, but all that'll happen is that they'll be interviewed, their alibis checked and then they're off the hook. They're hardly out of the way for long," Harry said.

"Okay, ties us up and diverts attention from the real perpetrators. How about that?" Jess said.

Jess could have something there. He beamed at her. "I think you've got it. Gold star, DS Wilde. Have we heard back from the lab yet? Anything on the PMs?"

"Both bodies have been formally identified and Melanie phoned to say we can see her and discuss the preliminary findings this afternoon," Jess said.

"Let's hope she's found something helpful."

"You had another call while you were out. Sandy Munroe. He wondered if we'd like to have lunch with him in the Crown, the pub across the road. Said he'd be there from twelve. What d'you think?"

Harry felt his stomach clench. This was only the beginning. "I think we're far too busy for pub lunches."

Jess smiled. "You never said he was coming down. He sounds nice."

"He is, but he'll have a reason for being here. My advice is don't get drawn in," Harry said.

"That reason will be you, Harry. He's worried about you."

"You've got that wrong. The reason he's here is because of your little tête-à-tête with Laing."

Jess scowled at him. "Blame me if you must, but you were really shaken up that day at the Reid. You heard a name and promptly threw up. What was I supposed to do? If you need help, then say so. And stop being so secretive. If you hadn't built up this big mystery around yourself, Harry Lennox, no one would be interested."

Harry couldn't listen to any more of this. He stalked out and went to get a coffee from the canteen. Jess had a point. Perhaps he should start talking about his past, tell her just enough to stem the torrent of questions. It might work.

Ten minutes later, he returned with a coffee and put it down on her desk. "Here, I forgive you. And you're right, you should meet Sandy, he's a good laugh, but perhaps later, once we've finished for the day."

Jess nodded. "What're we doing about Martha then? Do we pick her up or send a riot van?"

"We'll go, but we won't bring her in. I'll have a word with her somewhere quiet. I don't want to antagonise the woman any more than I have to."

Jess smiled. "And she likes you, don't forget that. By the way, Melanie's been on again, reckons she's found something. What's it to be, Martha first or what?"

"We'll do both. The Reid, and on the way back we'll call in on the Cassidys. Did Melanie say what she'd got?"

"No, only that it might help."

CHAPTER THIRTY-ONE

Dr Melanie Clarke had Sutton and Marsh laid out side by side on the morgue tables. "It's as I told you, both were suspended by the right arm for some time while still alive. The right shoulder joints are completely detached and there is extensive bruising. Both died from a single bullet wound to the head. The bodies have been cleaned, skin tests show a bleach solution, probably used to get rid of foreign DNA, but it wasn't used on the dismembered hands. Both men had bruised knuckles, the hands were dirty and there was oil under the fingernails."

"They put up a fight," Jess said.

Harry nodded. "They were hard men. If trapped, they would fight their corner. The oil — any joy with the Cassidy workshop?"

"No, that isn't a match, but I haven't done tests on the samples taken from the haulage yard yet," Melanie said. She held up her finger. "But there is something. I found this on Marsh's body." She pointed to Andy Marsh's cheek.

The white face with the waxy sheen of death looked unblemished to Harry. "What am I looking at?"

"What I think is a faint kiss mark," she said. "So far, all we have is that it is lipstick in a deep red shade. We'll do a full analysis and try to confirm the brand and the colour."

Harry was weighing up how this might help. So, a woman. All very well provided they found one who wore the same make. "What about DNA?" he asked.

"We'll try, but the sample is minute, and it has been degraded by the sluicing down in the container."

"Someone kissed him goodbye," Harry said.

"His wife?" Jess asked.

"I doubt it. Lisa is devastated. I can't see her being party to the murder of her husband in such a brutal fashion, but we'll speak to her again. We need a better picture of their relationship. For all we know, Andy Marsh was a womaniser, although we've heard no rumours."

"Anything else?" Jess asked.

"We're still testing," Melanie said. "Don't worry, we get something, you'll be the first to know."

"I'll add Lisa to the list," Jess said on their way out. "One thing we can be fairly sure of, that lipstick didn't come from Martha. Not her thing at all."

The idea of the tough, butch woman who wielded a wrench for a living wearing red lippy made Harry smile. "Who then? Not Martha, and I don't reckon Lisa. That doesn't leave us much to go on."

Jess shrugged. "Like you said, we'll just have to find out a lot more about Marsh's private life."

* * *

Harry felt strangely nervous about tackling Martha. Unusual, as it was normally personal problems that made his stomach clench the way it was now.

"It'll be fine," Jess said, glancing at his set expression. "She's hardly likely to attack you, is she? Martha's well aware of the consequences."

That wasn't a certainty. Say the wrong thing, give her a look she didn't like, and all hell could be let loose. "Wait here," he said.

They had stopped in the yard outside the Cassidy workshop. Despite the time, well after five, the place was still open. Harry could hear the radio blaring away inside.

"Martha, a word!" he called from the doorway.

She raised a pair of heavy-lidded eyes from the car engine she was working on. Harry sensed her gaze boring into him.

"What now?"

"A few questions, Martha. Nothing to get excited about."

She walked towards him, wiping her oily, calloused hands on a rag. "Go on then, ask away."

"Does the name Lancashire Holdings mean anything to you?" he said.

"Yes, it does. They want me to work for them."

Well, that was straightforward enough. "Have you met anyone from the company?"

"No, but I've had calls and a letter. They made me a good offer. A hefty upfront payment to show willing, and then we'll do regular work on their vehicles."

"What do they do, exactly? How do they make their money?" he asked.

With a shrug, she took a sheet of paper from a hook on the wall. "It says here long-distance haulage. I haven't asked them, why should I? I just accepted the offer straight off. I'm in no position to turn them down. Business is slow round here, folk have no money for car repairs and I've got a family to feed."

She handed Harry the sheet, which bore the Lancashire Holdings letterhead. It stated that the Cassidys would get paid the going rate for each job done as well as a monthly retainer.

"The bloke who rang me said the only condition is that they must get priority. They call, we repair. No waiting and no excuses. Tough deal, but there's not much else coming in, so what choice do I have?"

"What about the work you do for Craig Sutton? Surely that brings the money in."

"He throws us the odd bone now and again, just to keep the peace I reckon, but there's no way the work we get from him pays the bills. They have some firm in Stockfield that does the bulk of their work."

She looked strained. Martha might show the world a hard exterior, but she always did her best for her family. "Sorry, Martha, I didn't know things were that tight."

"Tight? I'll say they are. When I got the offer from Lancashire Holdings, I could hardly believe my luck. Saved our bacon and no mistake."

Harry knew that they'd chosen the Cassidy garage for a reason. And they'd offered Martha a deal they knew damn well she wouldn't refuse.

"The man who rang you — local, was he?" he asked.

"No, a foreigner. Couldn't tell you where from."

"Did you know they've attempted to implicate your Ryan in a bit of mischief?" Harry said.

It was obvious from the look on her face that she didn't. "What now? Our Ryan can get into enough trouble without needing any help."

"We're investigating a number of murders, Martha, heavy stuff, and every time we turn round, your Ryan's name appears. For a start, he's down as being this Lancashire Holdings' one and only director. The murders took place in a container belonging to them. What can you tell me about that?"

With a groan, Martha threw the spanner she'd been holding onto a metal bench, where it landed with a clang. "That'll be my fault," she admitted. "This bloke, the one who rang and sent me that," she nodded at the letter. "He wanted it that way. I didn't see any harm in it. I didn't know what they were up to, just haulage as far as I knew, like it says on there. He said our Ryan could have a good job once things took off."

"I believe they gave Ryan quite a bit of money. Does he know about your arrangement?"

"Ryan's a bit simple. I gave him the papers to sign and he did as he was told. That'll be what the money was for."

She looked worried, not like Martha at all. "Is he in trouble? He hasn't done anything, just gone along with what I've told him to do. If you have to arrest anyone, it'll have to be me. But I'm telling you now, I thought I was getting into a simple business arrangement, not murder. We both know my family has a reputation. Okay, the boys did a bit of thieving in the past but I put a stop to that. And I don't let them near drugs, despite what you might hear."

"I know this isn't down to you or your Ryan, Martha. You've been used. But I'll need your help to find the real killers. Are you sure he didn't give you a name?"

"No. I picked up the phone and he'd just say, 'Lancashire Holdings here.'"

"Is there anything you recall about his voice? Did you get the impression he was young or old?"

"Not from round here. Foreign like I said, but trying to hide it, and young, I guessed. Here," she shoved her mobile at him. "I've got the number logged as LH, you can copy it. But I doubt it'll do you much good, the call comes from a different number each time."

"The next time they get in touch, ring me," Harry said. "If they drop off a vehicle, don't let the driver leave until I get here."

"This is bad, isn't it? I've messed up and now we're all in danger."

"One step at a time. The main thing is to get the bastards, Martha."

CHAPTER THIRTY-TWO

Harry got into the car and slumped in his seat.

"That took you long enough. How'd you get on?" Jess asked.

"I think I've upset her."

"Martha Cassidy? You're not serious."

Harry heaved a sigh. "She's been conned into signing a contract with Lancashire Holdings. They gave her money up front, promised a monthly retainer and loads of work. Consequently, she believed they were offering her a good deal, and she sanctioned the use of Ryan's name as director. She's never met anyone from the firm. All the discussion was done by phone or letter."

"Has she given you any useful information about them?" Jess asked.

"Only that Lancashire Holdings are a haulage firm. The man who rang her was foreign she thinks. If he makes contact again or brings in a truck for repair, she's going to contact us."

"And that's it? But she's colluding with a gang of murderers, Harry. We should bring her in, question her further," Jess said.

"She knows nothing more that will help us. She told me the truth, I'm convinced of it. Martha and her boys have been used, end of."

"What now?"

Jess had an edge to her voice, she was frustrated, fed up of getting nowhere.

"How about we go for that drink with Sandy?" Harry said.

That cheered her up. "You're actually allowing me to meet someone from your past? Wow. I'm honoured."

"Just keep it general now, don't go getting too nosy," he said. "I'll give him a ring and we'll meet him in the Crown."

"Fine with me. Can't wait."

* * *

When they entered the pub, Sandy was already there, standing by the bar. Harry headed his way while Jess went off to the toilet. No doubt he'd be warning Sandy not to tell her too much, but Jess was determined not to be sidetracked. There was a Scottish angle to this case that hadn't been explored and Sandy could hold the key.

It'd been a difficult day. Left up to her, she'd have brought the Cassidys in and questioned the lot of them until they got something useful. Not Harry. He'd gone about things in his own way as usual. This was something he did a lot of, and Jess didn't always approve. She was afraid that one of these days he'd flout the rules once too often and drag her down with him.

She was about to return to the bar when she heard her name called. It was Sandy, he was standing at the open back door having a cigarette. She gave him a big smile and went to join him.

"Where's Harry?" she asked.

"Talking to that blonde barmaid," he grinned. "Don't worry about him, he won't notice we're gone."

"Time for introductions then. I've the dubious honour of being his sergeant, Jess Wilde," she said. "You, I'm told, are an old friend of Harry's."

"I am, I've known the lad since he was an infant. Harry speaks highly of you. How's the case going?" Sandy asked.

"It's a bitch and no mistake," Jess admitted.

Sandy grinned. "Any good, is he?"

Jess thought this was an odd thing to ask. "Harry is a good detective, but we've got a tricky case on our hands and we're not getting the breaks," Jess said. "What I'm waiting for is Harry to have a flash of inspiration."

"And if that doesn't happen, you make your own breaks, don't you?" Sandy nodded. "Believe me, the answers are there, you just have to find them."

Jess guessed he'd told his friend to keep his mouth shut. But she intended to try anyway, this was perhaps the only opportunity she'd get to talk to Sandy properly. "Actually, there is something you might help us with. We have a link to a Scottish villain but he's reluctant to run with it." She lowered her voice. "The weapon used to cut a victim's hand off had traces of flesh on it belonging to someone called Callum McBain. He's from up your way. D'you know anything about him?"

"I've heard a rumour that he's dead, not that a body has been found. I did know the man years ago. He was into all sorts of skulduggery. I heard he was mixed up with a gang of drug dealers." Sandy gave Jess a quizzical look. "Could that be an angle to pursue?"

"Possibly. The thing is, when McBain's name was mentioned the other day, Harry threw up. It was obviously a terrible shock to him. I'm afraid it'll do Harry's head in if McBain's enemies are somehow involved. We've got fatal overdoses, murder, and a haulage company whose owners are extremely secretive. The only individual in the frame currently seems to be European not Scottish. So, I don't understand how McBain got into the mix. But it does appear that whoever is responsible for the murders we're investigating also killed him."

"Look, hen, I'm having trouble hearing you above the din from the bar in there. Let's move into the garden, sit on that bench.

"I'd better check on Harry, if he finds us discussing him he won't be happy."

Jess walked back along the corridor and took a quick peek towards the bar. Harry had given up on the barmaid and was now chatting intently to an attractive dark-haired woman. Jess left him to it and went back to join Sandy outside.

"If I was you I'd forget McBain and concentrate instead on who might want him dead," Sandy said firmly. "The man was bad to the core and had a gang of thugs working for him, but his arch rival was even worse, a ruthless killer. It's possible he is at the bottom of what's happening on your patch now."

"But why come here? We're just an unimportant town with a very small market for drugs or anything else."

"The killer I'm talking about has old scores to settle with Harry," he said.

"How involved was Harry with this gang back in Glasgow?"

Sandy seemed to struggle with this. "Perhaps it's better that he discusses that with you himself."

"He won't," she said bluntly. "Harry likes to pretend that his past didn't happen. But clearly it did. I've seen his hands. He was in an accident, a bad one, and he's got the scars to prove it. He won't even tell me about that. What happened?"

"You should ask him. I don't want to talk about Harry behind his back. If he hasn't discussed it with you, he'll have his reasons." Sandy took a last draw on the cigarette and threw it to the floor. "It's up to Harry to tell you about his past. All I can say is the lad has issues. My advice is don't pressure him."

"Trouble is, I think Harry's past is bound up with our current case, and him not talking to me isn't helping us solve it."

"What I will say is that McBain got in the way of the vicious bastard I mentioned and that's why he'll have been killed. It's that man that haunts Harry, not McBain. But our lad in there," he nodded towards the bar, "is wasting his time. Rumour has it the man I'm on about is in hiding, but I have no evidence of that. What I do know is that he hasn't been seen in months."

"Are you talking about Mungo Salton?" Jess asked.

Sandy looked surprised that Jess had heard of him. "Yes, but for god's sake don't mention that name to Harry."

CHAPTER THIRTY-THREE

Day Seven

The following day, Harry woke to the sound of rain battering down on the van roof. Drips were coming through and splashing the clothes he'd dropped on the floor the previous night. Jess was right, he had to get somewhere else to live and quick.

And he'd drunk too much — again. Chatting up the dark-haired woman had cost him a fortune and got him nowhere. He couldn't even remember her name. Some huge bear of a man had turned up to collect her at closing time. As for Sandy, he'd spent his time getting to know Jess. Harry hoped he'd remembered his promise to lay off all talk of Glasgow.

Harry sat on the edge of the bed, his feet on the damp floor, and looked at the mess around him. This wasn't how he should be living. He earned a good wage, he'd had savings when he'd first come to Ryebridge, so what had gone wrong? His past, that's what, and the bloody memories that filled his head. Faces from his time in Glasgow swam through his dreams, most notably those of Salton and his own brother.

He was sinking again. At this rate he'd be back on the pills, and Harry didn't want that. He needed to get a grip, but even more important, he needed to sort this case.

A loud bang on the door made him jump. Clad only in his dressing gown, he went to see who it was.

It was a tall dark-haired woman. He squinted at her. He couldn't be sure, but he thought she was the one from the pub last night.

She smiled at him, looking him up and down. "Good morning, Mr Lennox. May I come in? Your weather is dreadful this morning and it is making me very wet."

A foreign accent. Why hadn't he noticed that in the bar? Too bloody drunk that's why. God, what was her name? And what had he said to her to bring her to his door at this time in the morning? It must have been an invite to breakfast.

"I have food, and coffee." She smiled again, entering the camper van and kicking the door closed with her high heel. She looked around at the cramped, untidy space and frowned. "You live like a pig."

"Sorry, I'd offer you a seat, but as you say . . ."

"You are a bad man. You live in a rubbish dump. But no matter, we will cope."

He watched her put the food on top of his one and only set of drawers. "I'm sorry. I know we spent some time chatting last night, but I can't remember much about it," he said.

"That is obvious. You do not even recall my name, do you? Which is a shame because soon we will become close."

Oh. Right. That cheered him up. She was certainly a looker and he must have made a good impression for her to bring him breakfast. She obviously fancied him. He gave her one of his cheeky grins. Things were looking up.

But seeing his expression, she tutted and shook her head. "You misunderstand, Mr Lennox. Charming as you are, I am talking business, nothing else."

Business? What was she on about? "Is this something we discussed last night? Because if so, I don't recall a thing."

She handed him a carton of coffee and a slip of paper. "I can see that. But no matter, it is something we will talk about now, over breakfast. Keep the paper safe, it has my mobile number on it."

Harry shook his head. "I'm sorry, but I'm in no position to go into business with anyone. For a start, I don't have any capital and I already have a good job."

"Not that good, obviously. Look at where you live. I know about the day job, and your lack of funds. I am here to put that right," she said. "Your job and your interesting past are what make you such a good proposition."

'Interesting past?' What did she mean? What did she know? The woman sat on a stool, sipping her coffee and staring at him coolly. She gave nothing away.

"I don't understand. If you know anything about me, you'll know I won't give up the day job, as you called it, for anyone."

"I'm not asking you to give it up," she said.

"Who are you?"

"Your new friend." She smiled. "And soon I will be your new employer."

Harry was about to put her straight when his mobile rang, breaking into the odd atmosphere. It was a frantic Martha Cassidy.

"You have to come," she said urgently. "We've got some maniac locked in our back room."

"What's happened?"

"It arrived this morning, a broken axle I reckon, although we've not had a proper look yet."

"What're you talking about, Martha?" Harry asked, keeping a wary eye on the woman.

"A bloody truck from them people, Lancashire Holdings. You said to ring if they turned up. Well they have, and my Caleb's scared witless. The driver, some foreign bloke, pulled a gun on him. My Caleb literally dodged a bullet and then managed to lamp him one. We've got him locked up in the back room. He's making a helluva noise. We took the gun and his mobile off him but he's trying to kick the door down and he's making threats. I'm not sure how long we can hold him."

"Don't worry, I'll alert backup and be with you soon. Do the best you can, but don't put yourselves in danger."

Harry turned to his visitor. "My job calls, I'm afraid. Fascinating as it is to talk to you, we'll have to leave the rest till later."

"Very well. I'll be in touch."

"Before you go, what's your name?"

"Emilia," she said. "I trust you won't forget it this time."

And then she was gone, leaving Harry with yet another puzzle. He wished he could recall last night's conversation but it was gone, evaporated like the fumes off alcohol.

CHAPTER THIRTY-FOUR

Harry arrived at the Cassidys just minutes after armed-response. Martha looked relieved to see him. She pointed to a metal door at the far end of the workshop. "He's in there. He was carrying a gun. That and his mobile are now in the drawer over there."

Harry put the mobile in an evidence bag and indicated to one of the armed officers. "Take it away," he said.

"We haven't touched the lorry," Martha said.

"I'll have it searched," Harry said. "You took a risk disarming him, you could have been shot."

"That was down to Caleb. He packs quite a punch when riled. The man threatened me, and Caleb saw red."

Harry joined Jess who had been hanging back near the main entrance.

"There's only the cab and the flatbed," she said. "If it was carrying a container, it's gone."

Harry had a shrewd idea where it would be parked. He pointed to the metal door. "Get him out," he told the officers. "Get him packed off to the station and we'll get round to Shaw's Haulage, see if the container is there. If not, we'll try Andy's old factory."

"Wonder what was in it," Jess said.

"And where it came from," Harry added.

Minutes later, forensics arrived from the Reid. "If you find any paperwork, bag it up," Harry said. He turned back to Jess. "A manifest would be useful, but I doubt we'll be that lucky."

They all stood back as the armed officers dragged a young man, kicking and screaming, from the locked room. He swore at them in some unintelligible language.

Harry turned to Jess. "Not from round here, then. Want to hazard a guess?"

"That's Urdu, and from the look of him, I'd say he was from Pakistan," she said.

Harry spoke to the armed-response team's commander. "We'll need backup for the next bit too. I suspect that lorry was carrying a container. We need to find it and deal with the contents."

"Which are?" the commander said.

"Afraid I've no idea. This lot and what they're up to are new to me."

* * *

"There was me thinking it would be a quiet morning, having a cosy chat with Lisa and getting the background on her life with Andy," Jess said once they were in the car.

Harry grinned. "But just think how much more exciting it is dealing with an armed villain. We'll speak to her later — first things first. We need to find that container. I want to know what this lot are up to."

"What just happened isn't funny, Harry. Martha and her boys could have been hurt."

"She wasn't though, was she? Canny lass is Martha."

"You take too many risks, Harry Lennox. Leaving Martha to deal with an incident like that—"

"I didn't. I told her to ring me if a lorry turned up."

"Well, turn up they did and were in a damn hurry from what she said."

"We find that container and go from there," Harry said.

"We could be stumbling into anything," Jess said.

"Which is why I've got armed response on our tails," Harry said. "What happened to you last night? I lost sight of you in the bar."

"I bumped into an old friend," she lied. "We did a bit of catching up."

"How d'you get on with Sandy?"

"He's okay, Sandy. I liked him."

"Did the pair of you get a chance to chat?"

"Not really, what passed between us was just about the job and how busy he is these days," she lied.

"Did you notice the woman I was with?" Harry said.

"Sophie?"

"No, a woman with long, dark hair. She was tall, had a foreign accent, though you wouldn't have heard that."

"Can't say I did," Jess said, "but the place was packed. Why d'you ask?"

Harry shrugged. "No reason."

Their first stop was Shaw's, the hauliers. When they arrived, they noticed a number of lorries and containers parked up. Harry and Jess went straight to the office and spoke to Roger Shaw.

"Have you had anything in from Lancashire Holdings in the last couple of days?" Harry asked.

"No," Shaw said. "They're blacklisted. But in any case, they haven't been back."

"You sure about that? There's a lot of lorries out there. I suppose you know where they've all come from?"

"Yes, they're all regulars," Shaw said. They thanked him and left.

"If not here, then where?" Jess asked on their way back across the yard.

"Andy's factory. Lancashire Holdings must have bought it with a purpose in mind," Harry said.

It turned out to be a good call. As they pulled into the car park, they could see signs of life. The lights were on inside, but the blinds were all down.

"Perhaps they're re-fitting the place," Jess said.

"I'm going to take a look," Harry said. "You wait in the car until the cavalry arrives, they'll soon be here. First sign of trouble, give them the nod."

Harry approached the building and hammered on the main door. If there was anyone from Lancashire Holdings in there, he wanted to get his hands on them first. "Police!" he shouted. "Open up!"

He could hear voices coming from inside and then the tip-tap of high heels on the wooden floor. The door swung open to reveal someone quite unexpected.

He blinked. "Emira?"

"As you see. What can I do for you?"

"Are you with Lancashire Holdings?"

"Yes."

"In that case, I need you to come down to the station and give a statement," he said.

But Emira merely shook her head. "I don't think so." She leaned forward and whispered, "Did you not listen to me this morning when I said you were going to work for us?"

This had to be a joke. These people were killers. Harry waved his badge at her. "I'm a policeman, a detective. If you think I can be intimidated or bribed, then you're wrong. You lot are prime suspects in two murder cases, possibly more. Those are serious offences and you will answer our questions."

She smiled and stroked his cheek. "You are very hand-some when you're angry, did you know that? But it's such a waste of energy."

Harry had heard enough. "You are coming with me now, Emira. You will be interviewed at the station under caution."

"I think not. You are in no position to make me or my partners do anything, Harry. Like I said, we know all about you."

Harry felt a sudden tremor of fear. What was she talking about? What did 'they' know? And who were they?

"What is it to be? I am busy, so make up your mind. But I seriously suggest that you tell your people this is a huge mistake and leave us in peace. Or . . ."

"Or what?" he said. "Go on. What do you think you know about me?"

The smile became a thin line. Her eyes were hard. "You are trying my patience. You had better do as we tell you, Harry. Or should I call you Paul?"

CHAPTER THIRTY-FIVE

"You drive us back, Jess." Harry got into the passenger seat. He was stunned by what Emira had just said to him.

Jess glanced at him. "What happened! Why aren't we dragging them in?"

"Mistake, Jess," he said. "I made a wrong call, so I told the cavalry to stand down."

"So, were they Lancashire Holdings or what?"

"No, just another clothing manufacturer setting up. They're refurbishing the place, like you thought."

"This property and the business were both bought by Lancashire Holdings, so what's going on? Where the hell are they then?"

Harry said nothing. He couldn't deal with this now.

"Fair enough," Jess said. "Perhaps they re-let the building, but we still need to find the container from the Cassidys' place. That lorry must have been carrying one."

Harry shook his head slowly. He couldn't get his head straight. If only Jess would stop wittering on. He had enough to think about without her questions. He had no idea what was going on, or how Emira knew what she did.

Receiving no response from him, Jess shrugged. "We'll set uniform on the job of finding it. Those things are too big to hide for long. And we don't know there was a container anyway. We're simply presuming there was."

Harry leaned back and closed his eyes. Emira must have spoken to someone, but who? He needed to speak to Sandy. Alone.

"Who did you speak to back there?" Jess asked. "I couldn't see."

"One of the admin people, I think. Look, Jess, I'm not feeling too good. Last night catching up. D'you mind if I go home for a couple of hours, get my head down?"

Jess gave him one of her funny looks. "Something's happened, hasn't it? One thing I do I know about you, Harry Lennox, you're no good at lying."

"I'll be back after lunch," he said, ignoring her comment. "Meanwhile, why don't you go and speak to Lisa? Find out what we wanted to know about her and Andy's story."

* * *

Harry rang Sandy from the camper van. "I need to see you. Where are you staying?"

"The Bluebell Guest House by the park. Great breakfast. I can recommend it."

"I'll pick you up in ten, don't disappear."

As he finished the call someone started hammering on the van door. "Open up!"

Standing outside was the young man Harry had met on the night of the riot at the Baxendale. "Zeno! I've been looking for you."

"Well now you've found me. In fact, I came looking for you." He smiled. "A lot's changed. Anyway, Emira says to give you this for a job well done. What she wants now is for you to release her driver. You have him locked up, I believe." Zeno held out a brown envelope.

Harry eyed it suspiciously. "What's this?"

"Like I said, a reward. You've earned it." Zeno turned to go. "Emira wants her driver back today. Don't let her down, she can be a vicious bitch when she's crossed."

Helplessly, Harry stood and watched him walk away. What could he do? Nothing, without starting a battle he would likely lose. And he didn't want that. It would mean giving up the job he loved. He looked inside the envelope. As he suspected, it was stuffed with money. Judging from the bulk, he reckoned about five grand. This couldn't go on. Grabbing his keys, he went to find Sandy.

* * *

"And that's what she said, Harry? Those exact words?" Sandy said.

"Yes, '*or should I call you Paul.*' She knows, Sandy. And I don't understand how."

Harry pulled into the deserted car park of a pub along the Stockfield Road. "We need to talk properly. This place is safe, there's never anyone here at lunchtime."

Harry went to the bar and got the drinks. Though he was driving, he got himself a whiskey. He needed it for his nerves.

"Someone has to have given her the information, laddie, and that could only be one person."

"Salton?"

"I'm afraid so. Apart from Salton himself, you, me and your twin, who's dead, no one else knew the truth about what happened that day."

"And McBain? I can only suppose he crossed Salton and suffered the same fate as Sutton and Marsh," Harry said.

"We don't know for sure that those killings were down to Salton or that McBain is dead. But it is his style."

"Do you really think Salton is behind what's happening on my patch?" Harry asked.

"Possibly, but I've heard no whispers. I'm going home later today, so I'll try to find out. If Salton is up to his old tricks, someone will know. Meanwhile, you must be careful. I don't need to tell you how dangerous he is."

"Think I don't know that? But what do I do? I don't want my past to come out. I've been careful, moving to a station in Yorkshire and then here. I've covered my tracks, told no one the truth."

"Don't panic. Sit tight for a day or so. Meanwhile, I'll try and find one of Salton's people, and when I do, I'll force the truth out of him."

"Don't take any risks, Sandy. I don't want you getting hurt for my sake. Morag would never forgive me." Morag was a cousin of Harry's mother. She and Sandy had been seeing each other for years.

"If it is Salton," Sandy said, "he'll make a move against you soon. He isn't known for his patience."

"I think he already has. I've been given a pile of cash. Salton's making it look like he's bribed me. This comes out and my career is over. He knows that," Harry said, dismay making his voice quiver.

"You need to calm down, laddie. Things aren't that bad. Keep the money safe for now and don't spend any of it, whatever you do. Don't tell any of your colleagues what's happened. Your super finds out and, like you say, he'll have your badge."

"I'm damn worried, Sandy. This is just what I've been trying to avoid ever since I left Glasgow."

CHAPTER THIRTY-SIX

Harry dropped Sandy off at the guest house and they said their goodbyes. "Let me know as soon as you find anything," Harry said. "I'm desperate."

"Leave it with me, laddie, I'll put the word out."

He should go to the station. The lorry driver was waiting to be interviewed. If he didn't show willing, his colleagues would think it odd, particularly Jess.

Harry decided to carry on as if nothing was wrong. He'd just have to stick the problem in a box in his head and tape it up tight. There was nothing else to do until he heard from Sandy. With luck, his friend would let him know what Salton was up to, and then he'd be on firmer ground.

* * *

Soon, Harry was talking to the duty sergeant, asking about what the driver had said so far.

"He won't give his name and there's nothing helpful on him," the sergeant said. "He's been making a helluva din and he's refusing food and drink. He's been offered a solicitor, but he's refused that too. He just says he wants to make a phone call."

"Did you manage to get prints and a sample of his DNA?" Harry asked.

"Yes, but it wasn't easy."

Harry had dealt with plenty of difficult suspects before, but the prospect of interviewing this one made him nervous. He'd have to tread very carefully. Emira evidently knew about him, but he'd no idea who else in her organisation did. The last thing he wanted was this man telling the entire station.

"I'll interview him with a uniformed officer. Make sure there's some backup close by. The man is obviously volatile."

Harry got himself a mug of coffee and despite his churning stomach, downed it in one. He'd just accepted a bribe — career over if anyone found out. "Which interview room is he in?"

"Number three."

Leaving the empty mug on his desk, Harry, with the PC beside him, made his way to the interview room. Their guest was shouting and screaming, but not in any language they understood. What had Jess said? Urdu? As soon as they entered the interview room, he turned on Harry, his eyes blazing with fury.

"You have made a mistake. You do not cross my people. Payment will be swift and deadly, I swear it."

"Dearie me," Harry said, taking a seat. "Threatening a police officer, eh? Not a good start. You have the right to a solicitor. D'you want one?"

"I will not be here that long."

"You're very sure of that. Do you realise that you've been arrested for a serious offence? Discharging a firearm at a member of the public carries a heavy penalty."

"No comment."

"Where did the lorry you were driving start its journey?"

The man's gaze burned, as if his eyes were on fire. "Go to hell."

"What were you carrying?"

"I will not talk to you. You were told to release me. Disobey and you will suffer."

Harry turned to the PC and rolled his eyes. "The lengths they'll go to."

"This is wasting time," he said to the driver. "I have no idea what you're on about. You've been arrested for attempted murder. I want to know why you were carrying a gun, and everything you know about that lorry. Bear in mind you committed a serious offence that carries a prison sentence."

"I will make that phone call now."

"We will do that. Give me the number and a colleague will relay a message."

"I want to speak to them myself."

"You do not have that right. Think yourself lucky we're informing someone for you," Harry said.

※ ※ ※

"Who did he want to call?" Harry asked back in the main office.

"Some bloke answered, said he'd get a solicitor here as soon as."

"Foreign?"

"Yeah, and not very talkative. I told him our guest was being held on a charge of attempted murder and that he shot at someone."

"It's lucky none of the Cassidy family was killed," Jess said, joining them.

Harry smiled at her. "Get much from Lisa?"

"No. She reckons they were sound and didn't like me insinuating otherwise." She stared at Harry. "You look bloody awful. Something happened?"

"Hangover," he whispered. "I tried to have that rest, but I had to see Sandy off. He's gone back home."

"Shame, I liked him. I still need to talk to Lisa. She kept saying her and Andy had been fine, but there was something, you know, a look in her eye. She really didn't like the idea that he might have been unfaithful. Want to come with me?"

"I have to stick around and see what our guest says once his brief gets here," Harry said. "It might be an idea to speak to Babs Milton. She worked with Andy, took his calls, saw who came and went. If he was up to something, she'd know."

"Good idea. I'll sort it."

Angela called out to him, "The solicitor's here, waiting for you in reception. They've asked for a word with you before the prisoner is interviewed again."

"I'll be right there. The sooner we sort this the better."

Harry took the stairs down to the ground floor. The solicitor should understand that there was no chance of bail, and that their client was as guilty as sin.

The duty sergeant pointed to a side room. "I've put her in there, sir."

He should have twigged then, but he didn't. He marched into the room, determined to get his own way, only to come face to face with Emira.

"You really don't learn, do you, Mr Lennox?"

"You are truly pissing me off now. Everywhere I turn, there you are. There is nothing I can do for your   your client."

She raised an eyebrow and moved closer to Harry. "He is one of my operatives, and you will have him released at once. Fail to do so and I will make your life extremely difficult."

Harry shook his head. "People witnessed what he did. He shot at someone. Luckily he missed, but I can't just let him go. That will cause far more trouble than your tittle-tattle, believe me."

"My tittle-tattle, as you call it, will finish you. So find a way," she hissed. "Speak to your witnesses and get them to change their minds. Bribe them if you must. I will give you the money."

Harry was about to challenge her again when Jess came in.

"Are you coming up? Our guest is getting very restless again," Jess said.

"Give us a minute, Jess."

Jess gave him one of her odd looks. She wasn't buying this at all.

"Go on. Leave us," he said.

Once she'd gone, Emira made for the door. "You have until midday tomorrow. If he isn't out by then, your chief constable will get a phone call." She kissed his cheek lightly as she passed him. "If that happens, you can say goodbye to your career, Detective Lennox."

CHAPTER THIRTY-SEVEN

Day Eight

Harry had hardly slept. He'd tossed and turned most of the night, trying to work out a solution to his problem. The only one he'd come up with was to tough it out. But supposing it didn't work? If they checked up on him, had he covered all bases? That, he decided, would depend on how rigorous those checks were.

There was a knock on the door, and he heard Jess calling his name. He'd have to let her in.

"Feeling better today?" she asked. "Good night's sleep and all that? Has it set you up for another day's sleuthing?"

"Yeah, I'm fine now," he lied. "Come in and make some coffee while I go and get dressed."

"Still living in a pigsty, I see. You really should get a grip, Harry. I'm not surprised you're not well, you could have caught anything in here. As for coffee, forget it. The mould in that mug over there is enough to poison an army."

"Leave it, Jess, this isn't the time." Harry couldn't face another earful right now. He disappeared into Don's house, had a quick shower and got dressed.

Ten minutes later, he was on his way back to the camper van when a man stopped him. He was tall, in his late forties and smartly dressed in a dark suit, white shirt and tie.

"DI Lennox?"

Harry wasn't in the mood for any more threats from Emira and her compatriots. "Who wants to know?"

"I do." The man held out a warrant card.

Still only half-awake, Harry thought the bloke might be from anti-corruption, that they'd finally discovered the truth, but the warrant said *National Crime Agency*. What in the world did that lot want with him?

"Would you like some breakfast?" the stranger asked.

Harry glanced towards the camper van. "My partner, DS Wilde, is waiting for me in there, I'd better have a word."

"No, don't do that." The stranger smiled. "Speak to her later. I won't keep you long. My car is parked down the road."

Harry looked to see if Jess was watching him from the window, but the curtains were still shut tight. "What was your name again? I'm still half asleep and didn't see the warrant properly."

"Marcus Edge," the man said. "I think you and me can do each other a lot of good."

* * *

Jess gave Harry twenty minutes and then went to look for him. What was the idiot doing wasting time like this? They had a busy morning ahead of them, not least that chat with Babs Milton. Banging on Don's door and shouting his name got her nowhere, though Harry's car was still parked up. Jess had had enough. She left for the station without him.

Back in the main office, Harry was not at his desk. "Have you heard from him?" she asked Angela.

"No, he hasn't rung in."

For a brief moment, Jess wondered if something had happened to him, perhaps he had fallen in Don's place. But she dismissed the thought. He'd have rung her.

"Have arrangements been made to interview the prisoner?"

Angela looked up from her computer screen. "No need. He's been released without charge."

Jess was stunned. What the hell was going on? Since when could folk pull a gun, use it in a public place and get away with it?

"I don't understand. What happened?"

"It was done on the super's orders. Apparently, you arrested the wrong man. It was all a big mistake."

It was no mistake. They had the gun and his mobile. If evidence was needed, forensics could provide the lot. "Try telling Martha Cassidy that," she said. She took her phone from her pocket and rang Harry. It went to voicemail. Now, why didn't that surprise her? What the hell was Harry playing at? What fairy tale had he told Rodders to get the shooter freed? And most of all, why?

CHAPTER THIRTY-EIGHT

Marcus Edge drove them out of Ryebridge towards Stockfield, and then towards a village up in the hills. "I know a café up here." He pointed towards a collection of stone buildings nestling against the hills. "It does a great full English."

"Look, I really haven't time to eat or the stomach for it. There's a mountain of work waiting for me back at the station."

"If you're talking about your gunman, that's all been sorted."

Harry stared at him. How could that possibly have been arranged? Marcus Edge had spoken so casually. "I don't understand. We had him banged to rights. It's only a matter of time before forensics find prints, as well as the bullet from the gun he used to shoot at Caleb Cassidy."

"Leave the details to me," Edge said. "The man is small fry in comparison to the ones we're after. The people who employ him think his release is down to you, and that's how I want it. You are now a valuable asset to them, and that makes you valuable to us too."

"I'm still not with you. Why would you want a man like that loose on the streets?"

"Don't worry, he's being watched."

Edge parked up in the café car park and they went inside. The place was empty. Edge nodded at the woman behind the counter, who seemed to know him.

"I'm not sure I can eat much," Harry said.

"As you please, but I'm starving," Edge said. "The full works, please, Claire." They sat down facing each other.

Harry settled for toast and coffee. "It does look great. I'll come back when I'm more up to it." He gave the man opposite him a long hard look. "What's this all about? You seem to possess the ability to work magic and it's making me somewhat nervous."

Marcus Edge laughed. "There's nothing magic about what I do, believe me. Right now, I'm slogging away on a bloody difficult case, just like you."

"I'm guessing it's the same one," Harry said.

Edge nodded. "I work in the Modern Slavery Human Trafficking Unit. It's part of the Organised Crime Command in the NCA. We coordinate with police forces in the UK and internationally to combat modern slavery crimes."

"Who is it you're after?"

"The man at the top, of course. Which is ambitious, even for us, as he has proved elusive so far. You see, this case is not as simple as you think. What you see, Harry, is merely the tip of an iceberg. These people operate all over the world, and what you're dealing with in your area is only a small part of it."

"Why would a worldwide operation be interested in our deprived little corner of northern England?" Harry said. "People round here have no money, most of them just manage to scrape a living together."

"Your patch has attracted some serious interest from people traffickers recently. What I'm after is names."

Harry stared at him. Drugs, yes, he'd seen that for himself. But trafficking? He'd seen no evidence of that. Then he twigged. "The container, the one brought in on that truck?"

"Exactly. That lorry travelled from Istanbul, crossed the channel, and ended up in Ryebridge. The cargo was people

— women and girls I suspect. Their destination, the clubs around the north west, the nail bars, the streets — you know the drill."

"What? All of them?" Harry gaped.

"No, some of them will remain in Ryebridge, one of them is valuable to them. I suspect they have something special lined up for her."

"Who are you talking about?"

"You'll have heard about the Tracy Buckton case, the missing heiress? We believe she is one of the women brought to Ryebridge in that container."

Harry was flabbergasted. That was a high-profile case that had been ongoing for months. Every station in the country had been alerted and sported a poster of the young woman's face on their notice boards. "What about the others?"

"Marsh's former factory is being transformed into a sweatshop as we speak. The women trafficked in will work at those machines until they drop. They'll get little or no pay, rubbish food and will be housed on that estate that gives you so much trouble."

"That was what they wanted the factory and Nick Sutton's houses for?" Harry asked.

"Yes. Naturally, Sutton and Marsh refused to hand their properties over. They were hard men in their own right and would have caused trouble, so they were got rid of. Nevertheless, these people like to ensure that the paperwork is in order." Edge laughed. "Hence, the factory was legally signed over for a pittance, as were the houses."

"And Sutton and Marsh lost their lives in the process," Harry said. "Now I'm investigating their murders."

"I know, and eventually you will get the guilty banged to rights. There was nothing I could do to stop the killings. At the time, I didn't have anyone in place to relay the information to me."

Harry was astonished that this man knew so much about what was going on. "Who is behind this? Do you have their names?"

Marcus Edge put down his fork. "I have a handful of names, Harry. Emira Mehmed and her brother Kamal for a start. It's their job to get things set up. It will have been one or both of them who murdered Sutton and Marsh."

Harry suddenly recalled the faint kiss mark on Andy's cheek. Emira had kissed him in the same way. Unconsciously, he touched his cheek. "I've met Emira but not the other one. Equally as, er, interesting, is he?"

"He's a huge monster of a man with no morals, every bit as vicious as his sister. When you do meet him, it's important you make him like you."

"Like me? I don't get it. I shall do my utmost to have nothing to do with him," Harry said.

"That might not be possible," Edge said.

"Why don't you simply arrest them? You appear to know everything, and you must have gathered sufficient evidence."

"Not that simple, I'm afraid."

"I don't understand what's stopping you," Harry said.

"What's happening in Ryebridge is a tiny piece of a much bigger enterprise," Edge said. "The Mehmets are helping to set things up here, but that's as far as it goes. They aren't in charge, and there is an entire hierarchy above them. The one I want is the man organising the operation across the whole of the north of England, not just around Ryebridge. Once he's in custody, I'm hoping to strike a deal and that he in turn will lead us up the tree, and eventually we will make serious inroads into the entire filthy business." Marcus Edge finished eating and studied Harry for a moment or two. "That's where you come in."

CHAPTER THIRTY-NINE

Harry was a definite no-show and Jess was damned annoyed with him. She could guess what had happened, he'd gone into Don's and instead of getting ready for work, he'd crashed out and was sleeping it off. Okay, if that was his game, she'd go it alone. When she'd spoken to Lisa Marsh yesterday, she hadn't learned much, later she'd go back and try again, but first she'd have another go at Babs Milton.

Babs had to know more than she'd told them. She'd worked closely with Andy, answered the office phone, was privy to his calls and probably his emails. It was possible that she held the key to a breakthrough.

Jess was nervous about visiting the Baxendale on her own, the place was a hotbed of crime and the youngsters were often keen to chance their luck against the police. She took a DC with her, Colin Vance. He knew the score, he'd even been on the sharp end of violence meted out by the Cassidys. His experience would make him doubly wary.

"We'll park up a few doors away," she told him. "The element of surprise might work to our advantage."

Once they'd parked up, Jess decided she'd approach the woman alone. "You stay in the car, out of sight. I don't want to worry Babs, nor do we want to upset the natives by appearing mob-handed. Spot anything suspicious, ring me and if I need you, I'll shout."

Jess didn't know a great deal about Babs, but she'd learned that Milton was her maiden name — divorced, attached, she had no idea. As she was about to get out of the car, she saw a man leaving the house.

"Get a photo," she urged DC Vance. "It might be useful."

"He's a bit of a brute," Vance noted. "Looks foreign, I'd say."

Jess felt a flutter of nerves. Vance was right. The man was tall and hefty with close-cropped hair. He got to the front gate, looked up and down the street, then took a mobile from his pocket and walked off, speaking to someone. Jess knew most of the troublemakers on the estate, but she'd never seen this one before. Was he a boyfriend, or was Babs being threatened? But she could see no reason. Lancashire Holdings had the factory and didn't appear to be making a play for anything else. Time to find out.

"A person can't get any peace round here anymore," Babs said. "I'm busy. What d'you want now? If it's information, I've told you everything I know."

"Who was that bloke who just left your house?" Jess asked.

Babs looked annoyed. "A bloody friend. Is that against the law?"

"I've not seen him before, that's all."

Babs chose not to elaborate. "Look, I've got stuff to do, so make it quick."

This time round, Babs was definitely not so friendly. She didn't even invite Jess inside.

"I'm still curious about the man who inquired about buying the factory," Jess said. "Have you remembered anything else about him?"

"Nothing to remember, love. Just some young bloke. Look, can't you get it through that thick skull of yours? I can't help you. I don't know anything."

"But you did see him. He kept bothering Andy, you said. Can you describe him?" Jess asked.

"Young, dark, foreign, I think. Oh, and he was well dressed." She glared at Jess. "But I've told you all this before."

Jess saw she was wasting her time. Babs wasn't going to say anything else. "Okay, but we might want to speak to you again."

"Any luck?" Vance asked when she was back in the car.

"No, but I feel sure she's lying. She's hiding something, I could see it on her face."

They drove off down the street. On the corner, Jess spotted the unknown man talking to some kids. "Pull over. Let's see what he's up to."

The pair watched the man grab hold of a young lad's arm, swing him off his feet and throw him to the ground. They were close enough to hear him swear, but he wasn't speaking English."

"I think that was Turkish," Vance said. "I speak a bit — comes off holidaying there every year."

"Who d'you reckon he is? A dealer perhaps?" Jess asked.

"Could be anyone. D'you want to bring him in?"

Jess was weighing that one up. There was just the two of them. She could call for backup, but what if the bloke was simply a parent out looking for his kid? They knew nothing about him, or what he was up to. Granted he knew Babs, but she was on the level too, as far as Jess knew.

"No, leave it. If he is a bad 'un, he'll make mincemeat of the pair of us."

Vance had his mobile out again and was taking photos of the man and the group of kids. "I'll check that little lot out back at the station."

The man took off again, back in the direction he'd just come from.

"Follow him," Jess said. "My gut tells me he's up to something."

"He might see us," Colin said.

"So what, he can't outrun the car, can he."

At the junction of Babs's road, he turned right into the street where Kelsey Green had lived. He stopped at her house and stood outside, apparently waiting. A quick phone call later and a minibus turned up.

"I wonder what's going on," Jess said. "What's he up to?"

The front door of the house opened, and a group of dishevelled-looking women and girls emerged. Some were dressed in western clothing while others wore eastern garb. Jess strained to see. She was sure some of them had their hands tied. They were shepherded out and pushed one by one and none too gently into the minibus.

"Get this videoed on your phone," Jess told Vance. "This isn't a bit of dealing, is it? This is something much worse."

CHAPTER FORTY

Harry shook his head. He didn't understand. "What use can I be? My work is limited to local crime. I don't know anything about the global, organised stuff."

This was way beyond what he wanted to get into. Harry had deliberately chosen to come to Ryebridge because it was the back end of nowhere, and crime here was the usual mix, with the occasional murder thrown in. What had been happening recently was way beyond normal for the area.

"Despite your reservations, you can be extremely useful to us. The local group have deliberately chosen you as their person on the inside, here in Ryebridge. As a senior CID officer, you have the power to turn a blind eye, in other words you can *make things go away*." Edge smiled.

"Why would I do that?"

"Because of what they know about you," Edge said

So, Edge knew about that too. Yes, Emira did appear to know things about him and she'd threatened him with that knowledge.

"I don't understand how they found out." And what did Edge know?

"They were told. You were selected as being someone who could be manipulated because of your past. That is how

165

they operate. In most areas across the country, in other countries too, they have people working for them in the police, in politics and in business."

"But I'm small fry. So is this town. It's of no importance to anyone."

"That makes it perfect for them. As I said, it's a crime-ridden area, has a population with little money, ideal for finding people who are easily bribed. That factory they acquired is now a sweatshop, but it will also be used for packaging drugs and as a front for the trafficking. From there, the girls will be hired out to clubs, pubs and beauty parlours, and they'll work for nothing. Some, particularly the pretty ones, will be sold on. It's a lucrative business, Harry, and these people operate all over the world."

"And there was me thinking it was all about the drugs."

"If it was, we wouldn't be meeting like this. The drugs aspect is not my remit. But drugs will be involved, doubtless transported along with the girls."

"How do they get hold of the women and girls?"

"The refugee camps on the other side of the Channel. Some are picked up at airports by men purporting to be taxi drivers. There are numerous ways."

This was an education for Harry. "And now they know about me. Do you know how that happened?"

"Mungo Salton is the prime candidate," Edge said. "We have information that he has been active in the Glasgow faction for the last year."

Given what he knew of Salton and what Sandy had told him, that made sense. Salton certainly hated him enough to stitch up the rest of his life. "I'd heard he'd disappeared. Gone absent for a while."

"He hasn't been seen for several months, that's true. He disappeared around the same time as McBain."

"So, what do I do now?" Harry asked.

"Nothing. You play along, Harry, do as they tell you."

Harry wasn't prepared for that. "You want me to become a bent copper?"

Marcus Edge smiled. "You already are. The gunman has been released and no doubt Emira has already delivered payment and is singing your praises. For the time being, I want you to do as she asks. But before you do anything, you must contact me, and I'll okay it. Your superintendent is aware of your position in case you become the subject of gossip in your station." He took a mobile from his jacket pocket. "Take this and use it only to ring me. It's a pay-as-you-go and it's unregistered. I will be using one the same. That way, should either of them fall into the wrong hands, it can't be traced back to us."

"Does this mean I'm working for the NCA now?"

"After a fashion. What we want from you is information. Emira, her brother and the lorry drivers are working for the man who runs the north of England, the one who orchestrates the entire operation. I want that man's name."

"There is someone else, a young man who goes by the name of Zeno," Harry said.

"Zeno is with us, working undercover. Well, he was. I've pulled him out. He's served his purpose."

A surprise. "He didn't say."

"And he won't," Edge said. "He wouldn't want compromising."

"Look, Marcus, you seem to have a lot of confidence in me. You believe I'm up to this, do you? You think that Emira or her brother will talk to me, tell me who is running the show?"

"You are up to the task, Harry. And Emira likes you. Gain her trust, be her friend. She is very much under the thumb of her brother, and that troubles her." Edge nodded. "Something for you to work on."

CHAPTER FORTY-ONE

Harry was back in the main office. "Sorry I'm a bit late," he said.

"A bit late? And that's it, is it?" Jess hissed. "Where the hell did you get to? I hung around yours for ages. I tried Don's door but I couldn't raise you."

"Like I said, I'm sorry, Jess. I'm still not feeling right."

"You're a bloody disgrace," she whispered. "And don't think I'm taking the flak for your sloppiness. You need to get your act together, Lennox."

If only she knew. Soon the gossip about him around the office would be much worse. He looked at the pile of paperwork on her desk. "What have you been up to anyway?"

Jess let out a deep sigh. "Do you want a blow-by-blow account or the skinny version?"

"Just the facts, Jess," he said.

"People trafficking. How does that grab you for a fact?"

Harry was stunned. This wasn't good. How had she got a handle on it so quick?

"That's what this is about," she said firmly. "The container, the need for accommodation and probably the factory too. Today, Vance and I watched about twenty females being taken away in a minibus from Kelsey's old house. What's the betting they've been put to work in Andy's place with no pay, awful conditions and made to keep at it until they drop?"

"How did you discover this?" Harry asked.

"Me and Vance paid Babs Milton a visit. She had a visitor, a rough-looking bloke, the type you wouldn't take on unless you had a death wish. We followed him and watched what happened."

"Perhaps it was simply a works bus picking people up," he said, knowing how lame that sounded.

"No, Harry." She was annoyed at his attitude. He should be pleased that they'd made some progress. "Some of the women had their hands tied. Take my word for it, they're being forced to work and when they're not slogging away, they're being held prisoner."

"Did you follow the minibus?" he asked.

"No. Chances are we'd have been seen and I didn't want to risk the women's safety. But it's easy enough to check out. Get a warrant and we'll search that factory, the houses too."

She was right, that was the correct thing to do. But he couldn't, not and keep Emira sweet. "Not yet. We need more evidence."

Jess stared at him. "What has happened to you? This isn't the Harry Lennox I know. The old you would be over there straight away and turning that place upside down."

"I'm working on another theory," he said.

"Care to share?"

"Not just yet, Jess."

"Hettie's been on, that brown envelope gave us nothing new print wise. Whoever handled it apart from Ryan must have worn gloves."

He left her and went in search of painkillers — the pack in his desk drawer was empty. That meant going down to the canteen. While he was there, he'd have a mug of coffee and a quiet think. Working for Marcus Edge was all very well, but it wasn't soothing his nerves any.

His mobile rang. It was Sandy. "Hi," Harry said. "Get home okay?"

"Yes, fine, laddie, and I've had a bit of luck. While I was away, another team in the station brought in a cohort of our friends. One of them is willing to strike a deal and he gave us some information. He confirmed that Salton is holed up on the Isle of Barra and running his operation from there."

"That's a bit far out. Why go there?" Harry asked.

"It is, but it does have a regular air service linking it to the mainland. He can be in Glasgow and back within hours. It's like I said, he'll be setting up an alibi. No one has ever been able to pin much on the man and he doesn't want it to start now. He's supposedly refurbishing a croft."

"A croft! That doesn't sound like Salton at all."

"My source is certain. Salton was in touch with his family just last week."

"Thanks, Sandy. I'll be in touch."

As he'd suspected and Edge had said, Salton was alive and well and still plotting. But was he behind what was going on here? Had he he. What had happened to McBain was proof of that. But where did that leave him?

* * *

"What's wrong with him?" Jess stared after him as he left the room. She couldn't understand Harry's reluctance to do what was right. "Colin, have you got anything from that film you took today?"

"The individual photos are a bit blurred — we were a distance away. But look at this."

Jess leaned over his computer screen. The video Colin had taken was sharp enough, particularly a shot of one of the women leaving the house and getting into the minibus.

"It's her, the blonde," he said, pointing to the image. "She was all over the papers, remember? She's thinner and the hair's grown but I reckon that's Tracy Buckton."

Jess shook her head. She was none the wiser.

"Daughter of Sir Ralph Buckton. She went missing last year while off backpacking. Got as far as Istanbul airport and was never seen again. You must recognise her, her photo has been on the noticeboard for months."

Jess felt such a fool. He was right. There was tons of stuff on that board, some important, some not, but usually it was just a blur of information and faces as she entered the office each morning. "Are you sure it's her?"

Colin enlarged the frame. "It's her all right. The case was headline news. I was just starting my career in CID at the time and for some reason, it grabbed me, so I followed it."

"This could be the break we need. If it is Tracy, she can give us valuable information. Get the file from the system. Let's have a proper look. And get stills from that piece of film printed out and blown up." She smiled. "I think you've got something here. Harry can't ignore this."

CHAPTER FORTY-TWO

Harry had to get word to Emira. Whether she liked it or not, he would have to follow up what Jess had told him about the factory, the house, and the women. Emira wouldn't like it, but if he was to keep his job, his reputation and continue to be useful to her, she would have to agree.

But first, he went out into the station car park and rang Marcus Edge for his advice. "There have been developments," he began. "My sergeant was at the Baxendale estate this morning and observed a group of women being taken away from one of the houses in a minibus. She wants me to organise a search of those houses as well as the factory."

"You have no choice, Harry. You'll have to get a warrant and do it. Contact Emira first and alert her so that she has time to empty them." He cleared his throat. "It's important that you behave normally, or your colleagues will suspect something. I'll be in touch. And if I may, I suggest you use this as an opportunity to get Emira on your side. She'll take it as a measure of your commitment and be grateful for your warning. She'll probably want to reward you. Make that work for you, Harry, invite her out, get to know her. We don't have a lot of time and we want that name. These shipments of people won't stop until we catch him. This week you're dealing with twenty women, next week there'll be twenty more, and you are just one small area. This is going on across the whole country, and we don't have the resources to keep tabs on it all."

But Harry wasn't happy with the arrangement. "I'm concerned about those women's safety, Marcus. They're on my patch, and they're my responsibility. Emira will have to hide them, and she may take risks with their lives. I'm not prepared to go along with that."

"Those women are worth money to Emira and her people. Believe me, they won't want any harm coming to them. But to be sure, I'll organise a watch on them."

Fair enough, if that's what Edge wanted. Harry took the scrap of paper Emira had given him from his pocket and called her.

"Harry, what is this? I told you to ring me only in an emergency."

"We have a situation, so listen up. We are about to search the factory and those houses you're using on the Baxendale. I don't have any choice in this," he lied. "The order has come from my superiors. You don't have long to cover your tracks."

"Why has this happened?" she asked angrily.

"One of your people has been a bit sloppy. Two of my colleagues saw him leaving Babs Milton's place earlier today. They didn't recognise him and were curious, so they followed him to a house we're familiar with. They saw the women come out of there and get into a minibus."

Emira muttered something unintelligible, which Harry presumed was a curse. "I will have it organised at once. You have done well and will be rewarded."

"No, it's okay. I don't need a reward. I'd much rather have dinner with you tonight. We can get to know each other better. What d'you say?"

"That is not my style. I do not socialise with my operatives," she said.

"What harm can it do? We could discuss how else I can help you. I'm a useful person to have on your side."

"You are a naughty man, Harry Lennox, but persuasive. I will consider it. If all goes well today, I will text and be at your place for eight."

Harry hurried back to the office and announced that they would do a blitz on the factory and the houses. "Get the warrant sorted," he said to Vance.

"We've found something else," Jess told him. "Come and look at this." She showed Harry the video footage of the women leaving Kelsey's old house. "This is down to Colin, by the way, he spotted it, not me." She froze the film and pointed at one of the women. "That's Tracy Buckton, heiress to the Buckton fortune. She disappeared last year if you remember."

Harry peered at the image. Since talking to Marcus Edge he did, and he'd read the updates. Naturally, he was pleased they'd found her, but it added a further complication. "Good work. Just as well you went with your instincts and followed that bloke."

"I've explained the situation to the magistrate," Colin said, phone in hand. "He's happy to rush the warrant, so I can pick it up right now if you like."

"Great. We'll organise the cavalry," Harry said.

"I've pulled the Buckton file," Jess said. "It looks as though whoever took her knew she'd be on that particular flight and was waiting for her when she landed. Her father has never come out and said it, but what's the betting he paid a huge sum of money to get her back. What d'you reckon?"

"If he did the money went for nothing. Tracy was never returned. Her parents must have been distraught," Harry said. "The updates amounted to very little. The girl disappeared off the face of the earth. It was suggested that she'd run away, perhaps with a boyfriend, but her parents refuted that."

"Sir Ralph has never given up. He appeals to her kidnappers on a regular basis, offering more money each time. For all we know, the kidnappers or traffickers could be bleeding him dry."

"This is grim, Jess. That girl obviously didn't run away from home. She has been kept prisoner, and we can only guess at the conditions. The others too. The sooner we get them out, the better."

She smiled at him delightedly. "Thank goodness. That's more like the Harry I know and love."

CHAPTER FORTY-THREE

Getting the warrant took longer than they'd expected. The magistrate was in court, hearing a case, so they had to wait. Finally, after an hour or so, Harry got the paperwork.

By the time he brought it to the station, Jess was losing it. She had spent the entire hour pacing up and down the office.

"We should have gone hours ago," she complained.

"Calm down, we needed the paperwork. We have to do it right. We'll hit both targets at once, and armed support will back us up. These people aren't playing games."

Jess nodded. "You take the factory, me and Colin will do the houses. But we'll take the biggest number of officers, there are five houses to search."

"Okay by me," Harry said.

That meant he would be with a group of uniformed officers, which suited him fine. Any problems and they wouldn't notice odd behaviour on his part. Whereas Jess definitely would.

"The minute you're clear, ring me," Harry told her.

A PC accompanied Harry in his car. He was keeping everything crossed that Emira had had enough time. And it looked as if she had. When they arrived, he was relieved to see the factory car park empty, with no sign of a minibus.

176

"We need to get inside," he said, and ran to the main door, banging on it hard. "Open up!"

A PC approached carrying a battering ram. "Don't worry, sir, we'll soon have it open."

They were about to force their way in when they heard someone whistling inside. Seconds later, the doors swung open and a small woman wearing overalls stood looking up at them.

"Give me a chance," she said. "I was mopping the floor in the back room. What d'you want? There's no one here but me."

The PC who'd come with Harry pushed past her. "There has to be. Where is the workforce? The women? We had solid information that they had been brought here."

Harry leaned back against the wall and sighed. "In point of fact, we didn't. Our colleagues didn't actually see that bus come here at all."

"Waste of time?" the PC said.

"I reckon so." Harry shrugged. "But we'll have a quick look round while we're here."

"Help yourselves, but there's nowt to see. They're still setting up," the woman said. "They're hoping to get started next week."

She acted the part well, Harry had to give her that. "And you are?"

"Mildred Smith. I've been cleaning here since Mr Marsh's day. I'm lucky, they've kept me on."

She was lying, Harry felt sure of it. "Okay, thanks. We'll get on and leave you in peace."

And the factory was just as it had been — same machines, same layout. Emira had worked hard to get everything sorted in time.

"Let's hope the others have more luck," Harry said.

* * *

Jess had the front doors of all five houses open within minutes of their arrival, and the uniformed officers quickly set about doing their search. Three were empty, stripped of all furniture and in a state of disrepair. The other two were obviously undergoing refurbishment.

She stood in Kelsey's former home and looked around her helplessly. "I don't understand. We were here not long ago, yet these properties look as if they haven't had anyone in them for ages."

"I've found this, ma'am. It was lying over a chair in the next room. It's covered in mud and pongs a bit." One of the PCs was holding out, at arm's length, a tatty woollen jumper.

"Bag it," Jess said. "We might get DNA." But she wasn't hopeful. Most likely it had belonged to one of the homeless guys.

"No sign of the trafficked girls," Colin said. "What the hell's happened?"

"We know what we saw," she said. "This isn't right. There should be evidence of people living here. Beds, mattresses crammed into every spare inch of space. But there's nothing."

"They've been tipped off," Colin whispered. "What's the betting it's the same at the factory."

Jess was furious. How had this happened? They'd seen those women, they had video footage, so what had gone wrong?

"Your mobile's ringing," Colin said.

It was Harry. "There's no one here but the cleaner and she's no threat. You really should have followed that bus, Jess. This has been one huge waste of time."

"Same here. This is all wrong, Harry. We saw those women leave this house and get onto that bus. Where else could they have been taken?"

"No idea, but not where you thought," he said. "Not Marsh's factory that's for sure. I'm calling it."

Jess let out a groan of frustration. Had someone seen them earlier and tipped them off? Unlikely as it seemed, that was the only explanation, yet Jess wasn't convinced. "Something's wrong, Harry. We've been stitched up."

"Did you get anything at all from the houses?"

"No, unless you count one mucky old jumper."

"Bad deal all round then. Meet me back at the station. We'll have to file our reports and they won't make comfortable reading for the higher-ups."

As far as Harry's credibility with Emira was concerned, all was well, but he still had a huge problem. Jess had definitely seen those women. They weren't here or in those houses, so what had happened to them? He could only hope that Edge had kept his word and knew where they'd been taken. And that Emira hadn't done anything rash in her haste to clear up.

CHAPTER FORTY-FOUR

"We're in luck, Rodders has left for the day," Jess said.

"So, we face the flak in the morning," Harry shrugged, "To be honest, Jess, I'm too knackered to care right now. I'm calling it a day."

He grabbed his stuff and left. That could have been one tricky situation, but he'd managed to swerve it and stay in Emira's good books. Would she turn up tonight? If she did, it was his chance to find out what she'd done with those women, and who was running the show.

On his way back to the van, he got a text from Emira. Tonight was on. He needed to get himself ready, ensure he looked the part. There was a quiet little restaurant in Hurst that he'd earmarked as a likely contender. He'd been there before and not bumped into anyone from the station, which made it a perfect venue.

Don was working away from home for the next couple of days, so he had the place to himself. He used Don's shower and borrowed some of his more expensive clothes. Luckily, both men were the same size and Don had excellent taste. Studying his reflection in the full-length mirror, Harry had to admit he didn't look half bad, even if he was his only fan.

Walking back across the drive, he spotted Emira getting out of a black saloon. The driver, the same brute of a man who'd picked her up in the Crown the other night, was screaming at her and shaking his fist. Kamal, Harry presumed.

"You okay?" he said, hurrying over to her.

Kamal, if that's who it was, had driven off at speed.

"Kamal, my brother. The idiot thinks he owns me." She leaned forward and kissed his cheek. "But he doesn't. I am my own woman. He has a lot to learn."

Harry nodded and led her towards his car. "I'll just pop in and get my wallet. I thought a meal, a little wine? What do you think? Call it a chance to chat and get to know each other better."

The van was a tip, there was no way he could invite her in here. His wallet was on the seating unit, but he couldn't find his mobile. Shifting a few things about, he eventually retrieved it from under a cushion. He'd missed a call from Martha. What did she want? He should ring her back, Martha wouldn't ring unless she had a good reason. But a glance out of the window told him that Emira was getting restless. Martha would have to wait. He'd call her back later.

* * *

"I really did not expect you and me to be friends," Emira began. They were seated at a corner table, a bottle of wine in front of them. "Especially since I coerced you into joining us. The candidates we select from your line of business are usually a little more . . . reticent."

Harry smiled back and took her hand. "You caught me at the perfect time. Don't misunderstand me, I enjoy being a cop, but so far it has given me precious little, not even job satisfaction. My lot is late nights, weekends that don't exist and an empty bank account. I was thinking about ways to put that little lot right, and suddenly, there you were."

Emira laughed, her dark eyes sparkling in the low lights of the restaurant. "Then we are not that different, me and you. I too have often wondered how to get out of my own situation. But, unlike you, I am not hiding a dark secret and I can't be easily blackmailed."

Harry laughed. "Oh, it's not that dark. And as for being easily blackmailed, what about your little secret? People trafficking is very much frowned upon in police circles."

"Your secret can do you more harm than mine can me, I think." She gave him a sly smile. "Tell me, Harry, which of your colleagues know about you? I'm guessing none of them, and that is your weak point. It's what has given us a way in."

Harry bristled, but forced a smile. She was right, but he had to steer the conversation back to her, away from him and his past. "You want out, you say. Why? You seem to have it all. You've got the police in your pocket, money, and you're your own boss."

She laughed and shook her head. "That is not true. I have to do as I am told, just like you. But unlike you, I break the rules and I love more than my job."

Harry understood what she was saying. She was afraid, he saw it in her dark eyes. "Sorry, I thought you were the one in charge."

"Well, I am not."

"But you know who is. Your brother?"

That seemed to amuse her. "Kamal? Oh no. He is a mere minion. He does as he is told, and he's terrified of getting it wrong. If he does, they will kill him." She sipped her wine. "The people we work for count life cheap, Harry. Both Kamal and I have a lot to be scared of."

"I've seen some of their handiwork." He grimaced. "How did you find out about me, and my, er, weakness?"

"I was told. Not the details. Simply what to say should you prove difficult. I'm glad it worked. I would not like to see you get hurt, Harry Lennox."

"It was the name that made me curious. Aside from you, there's only two other people that know about Paul."

"That's enough," she snapped. "You are trying to get information I am not allowed to give. I tell you about the people I work for and I will not live to see tomorrow. Anyway, you are wasting your time, I have no names to give. That is how our organisation works." She looked away. "But know this. You must take care, the boss is a wicked man, a killer who makes use of any advantage that presents itself. I do not intend to be one of his victims, so you can stop this interrogation right now."

She obviously wasn't going to tell him any more about the boss, so Harry decided to drop it. He changed the subject. "You did well today, you got things organised at the factory and the Baxendale pretty fast."

She smiled. "How do you say it, by the skin of our teeth. We, I, owe you for the information. Had those women been found, I would have been killed. They are valuable. One in particular is worth a fortune and I know there are special plans for her, and as I said, my boss doesn't tolerate failure."

Harry nodded as if in understanding. So, Emira was every bit a prisoner as those women, except that her role was a little different. He wondered if she, too, had once been trafficked.

"What did you do with them in the end?" he asked.

She wagged a finger at him. "Uh-uh. You are very naughty. You know very well that I cannot tell you. You ask too many questions. Today has delayed proceedings, and I have to get things back on schedule fast. You can help with that. There are still policemen watching the houses and factory. You must remove them so that operations can resume."

Harry started to speak but his mobile buzzed. It was Martha Cassidy — again. "I'm sorry, Emira, I'll have to get this."

"Can't it wait?" he barked into the phone. "I'm in a meeting."

"No, it bloody can't. You need to get your arse round to my yard. Someone's dumped a container here and there's a helluva lot of wailing and screaming coming from it."

CHAPTER FORTY-FIVE

Harry glanced at Emira. That could mean only one thing — the women. They must have been put back in the container that brought them into the country to wait until it was all clear to return them to the houses. Why hadn't Marcus Edge alerted him to their predicament? Harry got up and moved out of earshot of Emira.

"Have you told anyone else?" he asked Martha.

"No, but if you don't do something, I will. I'll be ringing the local cop shop."

She would too, and Harry didn't blame her. Those poor women must be scared witless. "What are you doing working at this time of night?"

"Never mind that, it's a bloody good job I am. Those poor sods won't last long without food and water and it's freezing cold. There's no heat in them things."

She was right. Harry must alert his colleagues and get those women freed at once. He looked across at Emira, toying with her wine glass. How could she allow this to happen? She had to know what had been done with them, and the inhumane conditions they were being kept in. Okay, she was tied to the gang, but still, the woman couldn't have an ounce of humanity in her. She had sat here, happily wining and dining, having left those poor sods in the cold and dark wondering if they'd ever get out.

Marcus Edge could stuff his undercover job. He'd failed to keep those women safe. He'd promised to have them watched, but he hadn't. All that mattered to him was the operation and using him to get a name out of Emira.

"I'll sort it, Martha. We'll get them out. It won't be long."

He went back to the table and threw down fifty quid. "We've not eaten yet, that should cover the wine. Get yourself a taxi, I've got to go."

"Wait! Harry," she called after him, "it's still early, we have things to discuss . . ."

But Harry was gone. Outside the restaurant, he got on his mobile and called the station. "Cassidy's yard," he told the duty sergeant. "Get a team round there and alert social services or whoever. There is a container there with a number of trafficked women in it. They'll need taking somewhere secure and looking after."

Next, he rang Jess, who said she'd meet him there.

* * *

By the time Harry arrived at Martha's yard, Martha and Caleb had forced the container doors open. The team from the station were there. The women, about twenty of them, were standing huddled together, looking terrified.

"Some of them are young," Jess confirmed. "A couple are no more than fifteen, I'd say. I haven't heard much English spoken, so it's difficult to work out what happened."

"I can tell you." A young woman came towards them. She had a blanket around her shoulders, her long blonde hair was straggly and she was frighteningly thin. "I'm Tracy Buckton. I was kidnapped about a year ago."

"Tracy!" Jess put an arm around her. "It's okay, you don't have to say anything yet. We'll get you somewhere warm and safe, and you can talk to us in the morning when you're rested."

185

"You must tell my dad I'm safe. He'll be out of his mind with worry," Tracy said. She sounded infinitely weary.

"DI Lennox?" A woman approached and showed him her ID. "I'm Bernie Stafford from Social Services. I've arranged somewhere for them to go for tonight. Tomorrow, I'll contact the appropriate agencies and we can go from there."

Harry nodded, and watched as the women were helped into several vehicles. "I want to know where they are at all times," he said to Bernie. "I'll arrange for them to be guarded. The people who took them are dangerous, they consider the women to be their property and will want them back."

"Here." She handed him a card with an address on it. "Your men can follow us."

"Martha's not so bad after all, is she?" Jess said, once everyone had dispersed.

"No, she's not. But she's crossed some dangerous people. We need to ensure that she and her family are safe too." He looked at Jess. "There will be repercussions from this. It'll change things."

"What're you talking about? We've got them back, we've done good." Jess looked him up and down. "Oh. Did Martha disturb something? Date night was it?"

"Something like that, but don't jump to conclusions, it was work."

"What work, Lennox? And how come I didn't know about it?"

"Because I'm keeping you out of it for your own good."

He walked off. He needed to get back to the camper van as soon as. He had a bad feeling about what would happen next. It had been a relief to find the women and have them safe at last, but Emira's people wouldn't let things lie. They would demand their pound of flesh.

Harry decided to find somewhere else to bed down for the time being. The van wasn't secure, and he didn't fancy having his throat slit in the middle of the night. He'd pack a few things and find a bed and breakfast. He was about to turn into Don's drive when an explosion rocked the car. He saw flames leap into the night sky, and the camper van was suddenly a ball of flame.

This was no accident. The fire had been meant for him.

CHAPTER FORTY-SIX

The Bluebell Guest House had been good enough for Sandy, so Harry would try there. He had nothing but the clothes he stood up in, and those belonged to Don. First thing in the morning, he'd have no choice but to go and ask Anthea for his things back.

"Will you want breakfast?" the receptionist asked him when he checked in.

Harry nodded. Why not? After all, Sandy had recommended it. Once he was in his room, he took off his jacket and shoes and rang Marcus Edge. Fortunately, he'd had the burner phone in his car with him.

"We have a problem," Harry began, "and all because you didn't do the job right. You said you'd keep an eye on those women, so what were they doing in that bloody container?"

"Sorry, it wasn't possible. These people are clever. They were taken away in several vehicles, driven all over the place, and we couldn't keep track of them all. Your department isn't the only one on a tight budget, you know."

A poor excuse. "You didn't try, did you? This was another ploy to push Emira at me. Keep those women stashed away out of sight until I clear the watch on the factory and the houses, which would put me high on the list of Emira's favourite people. Well, it didn't work. Emira isn't going to talk, she's far too scared. You gained nothing from this, Edge, except to put those women at even more risk."

"The women weren't in any danger, they were simply hidden. Like I told you, they're too valuable to be harmed. My people did their best, Harry, but we don't have unlimited resources. No one was more annoyed than me when I learned they'd lost them."

"Well, I don't want anyone else putting in danger, is that clear?"

"Perfectly, but the one currently in danger is you. Our friends won't be happy about losing the women. They'll blame you and they'll want payment."

Harry chuckled. "Let them ask. I've nothing left to give. They've as fin in the camper van, I'm homeless and I have no belongings either, nothing."

Marcus Edge ignored that. "Did Emira tell you anything?"

Hadn't he listened to a word? All Edge seemed to care about was getting whoever was running this operation. "No, she clammed up. I don't think she'll ever talk. Don't ask me to try and wear her down either, it would take for ever. The woman is as hard as stone. Those trafficked women were left in a container. Had we not freed them, god knows how long they'd have been there."

"You have to keep her onside, Harry. Emira won't let this go. Walk away and she'll talk. About you, Harry."

"She knows nothing. All she had was a few words she'd been given to use on me."

"The loss of those women will hurt. It'll mean lost revenue and you will be blamed. Your position is compromised."

"What, as your spy?"

"No, as a CID officer," Edge said.

"But that's what I am."

"Are you sure?"

"You trying to blackmail me too, Edge? You're no better than them."

It was several seconds before Marcus spoke again. "If accusations are made there'll be checks, and who knows how robust those will be. If the force want to find you out, they will."

Harry felt his stomach flip. He didn't want this, but what could he do? "You're probably right. Any suggestions?"

"Try again. Ring her. Tell Emira a colleague found the container and you had no choice but to go along with it. Promise to help get the women back."

"I'm the DI in charge of the case. She's an intelligent woman, I can't see her buying that."

"Pour on the charm, Harry. They need you, remember." Edge finished the call.

Harry lay back on the bed, wondering if he was right. He closed his eyes. This wasn't what he'd signed up for. Edge had no idea. Harry knew if he'd been in that camper van earlier, he'd have been fried.

His mobile rang. "Yes?"

"Harry, you are okay? You are not hurt?"

It was Emira. So, she must know about the attempt on his life. "Checking up to see if I'm dead, are you?"

"No, of course not. I had no idea what Kamal was up to."

"He tried very hard, believe me. A few minutes later and I'd have been toast."

"Kamal is angry about the women and blames you. He blames me too. He says I have treated you too leniently. He says you are a threat, can't be trusted. He wants you dead, Harry."

Harry had put that much together himself. So much for them needing him. "And you? What d'you want, Emira?"

"Like I told you, a way out. But if I speak to you, Kamal will kill me too."

Harry sat up. "But you're his sister. He won't harm you, surely?"

"He has before. I have the scars to prove it."

"I'm sorry, I had no idea."

190

"Harry, we should help each other. That way, we can rid ourselves of this situation."

Was she on the level? "How do we manage that?"

"Kamal wants to broker a deal. Give him back the women, he will let me go and give you money. Me too, so that we can build new lives."

"And if I refuse?"

The line seemed to go dead, then he heard muffled sounds, followed by a scream. Emira

"You have been offered a way out, imbecile, now take it!" a rough male voice rasped at him. "Refuse and I will kill you. Her too."

Kamal! Harry had to offer him something. He didn't want Emira harmed, so the quicker the two of them were brought in, the better. "Okay, what are your terms?"

"You will tell me every move those women make. The authorities will speak to them, no doubt there will be hospital checks. The minute they leave your protection, you will tell me, and I will arrange to get my property back. I do not have long. Next week there will be another shipment." He paused. "I will not stand for any further interference, do you understand? Tomorrow, I will give you one of my operatives. He will confess to the trafficking and you will close the case."

Harry agreed, to give himself time. He'd no idea how this was going to work. Apart from questioning the women, it was unlikely he'd have any say in what happened to them, or where they were taken. Kamal would have to be trapped and caught some other way.

191

CHAPTER FORTY-SEVEN

Day Nine

Anthea stood on her doorstep, arms folded, her mouth pulled into a thin line. "Harry, if this is some ploy to wheedle your way back, you're wasting your time. We're done."

"I know. I've accepted that now," he said. "But can I have my stuff, please? Some idiot set fire to the camper van I was living in, and I've got nothing left." He saw the look of disbelief. "Don's van," he explained, "the one parked on his drive. That's where I've been living these last weeks."

That expression was still there. She didn't believe a word.

"You look smart enough to me. Are you telling me the truth?"

"These clothes are Don's too. I had to go to a function last night, so I borrowed them off him."

"Okay, the stuff's no use to me anyway. Everything belonging to you is in the shed. I'll get you the key."

"Thanks, Anthea."

"I'll open the side gate so you can come round. Make sure you clear the lot. I don't want you coming back. We're finished, Harry. Have you got that straight?"

He didn't need telling twice, the look on her face was enough. Another relationship down the drain, but it was no more than he'd expected, and probably no more than he deserved. He'd never been there for her, and it wasn't always down to the job. He'd often used the late hours as an excuse to get out of occasions involving Anthea's family and friends that didn't interest him. The break-up was his fault, no excuses. In fact, Anthea deserved a medal for putting up with him for so long.

There were three suitcases and a box of books, photos and stuff. Not much to show for his thirty-five years. But at least he had something to wear now. He piled it all in the boot of his car and made for the station.

During the drive, he thought about the case and tried to work out a plan. Kamal wanted the women back, but he couldn't let that happen. If he made contact today, he'd have to find a way to keep him busy with something else.

"Marsh's car has turned up," Jess told him as soon as he entered the main office. "Not much help though, it was well burnt out. It was found on the spare ground at the back of the park. Forensics will take a look but there's not a lot left."

"How come it's taken this long to find it?"

"Some of that area is dense woodland, it was in among the trees."

"So, they made sure there was nothing left to help us."

"And some."

Harry could well imagine. It sounded like Kamal's work, he was good at setting fires. "The camper van was set alight last night."

Jess jumped to her feet and went to his side. "Are you all right? You're not hurt or anything?"

"I'm fine, but only because I wasn't in it at the time."

"What happened? Was it an accident or what?" she asked.

"No, it was meant to kill me. I've upset someone — the traffickers I suspect. Rescuing those women sent someone over the edge."

"We'll interview them today, see what they can tell us. Most of them will require an interpreter, but Tracy will be okay. She's a clever girl too. I had a few words with her this morning. She remembers a lot about what happened to them."

"Names would be good," Harry said, helping himself to coffee from the machine.

"Where did you sleep? Don's?"

"Didn't want to chance it in case they came back. I've done Don enough harm by getting the van trashed. I went to that bed and breakfast Sandy used. It's okay, not too bad at all. And I got my stuff back off Anthea. I think she felt sorry for me." He laughed.

"But you can't stay in a B&B indefinitely, it'll cost you a fortune."

He sat down at his computer. "Don't worry about me, Jessie, I'll find somewhere."

"Forensics have sent the report through regarding the oil on Marsh's and Sutton's hands," she told him. "It's a match for what we got from the ground at Shaw's Haulage."

"Fair enough, it's as we thought. They must have fought with their attackers in the yard. They both had bruised knuckles, remember. Anything else?"

"Yes, and this is the bit I can't get my head round. Hettie finally looked at the soles of those shoes of Lucy Green's. There is a DNA match, so they were definitely hers."

That was conclusive proof that Kelsey had known where her daughter was. She bought the shoes after she disappeared and they were the ones Lucy had on her feet when she was found. "Anything interesting?"

"She found traces of exactly the same oil as on Marsh and Sutton's hands."

Harry stared at her. "How can that be?"

"I've been trying to work that out for the last hour. Lucy must have been there. It's not just the oil, there's also traces of the stone that covers the parking area, and what we think is chicken feed of all things."

"Chicken feed?"

"I've no idea, but do you remember that when we first met Lucy, she kept talking about a 'Clara cluck-cluck?' That could have been a chicken. Perhaps the people who took her kept chickens."

CHAPTER FORTY-EIGHT

Tracy Buckton looked marginally better than she had the night before. Gone was the frightened, cowering girl but her face was still haggard and she was painfully thin. But she had regained a certain amount of confidence. Tracy wanted to help, to get justice for herself and the women she'd been imprisoned with.

"That was the first good night's sleep I've had in ages. The best part was the quiet. There was no one crying." She smiled. "For the first time in months, I can see a way forward."

Harry beamed back at her. She was young, just twenty according to the files. And she was obviously bright. He had high hopes of Tracy. "What can you tell me about the men who took you?"

"The day I arrived in Istanbul a taxi dropped me off at the hotel. I was about to go inside and check in when a man stopped me. He said he worked for my dad and had come to tell me he'd been taken ill and needed me at home. The man offered to take me straight back to the airport." She shook her head. "I was completely taken in. The only thing I could think about was dad being sick. I tried ringing home but got no response. The man said not to worry. Dad had been taken to hospital. I was about to call them, but the man said we had to hurry if we wanted to make the plane in time. I can't believe I was taken in so easily."

She was on the brink of tears. Jess offered her some water. "Take your time, Tracy. You're doing great."

"I got in his car and he drove out of the city. After that it all becomes a bit of a blur. He gave me a bottle of water, which must have been drugged. I have no idea how many different vehicles I was forced into, but it was a lot. Eventually, I found myself in a beat-up van with four other women."

"Did you get to know anything about them?" Jess asked.

"Yes. They were young, like me, and western. One was French, the other two were from Spain. We seemed to travel for days before we arrived at a villa by a beach. I have no idea where it was, but it was a beautiful place, lavishly done out and very busy. People were coming and going all the time."

"Why? What did they want from you?" Harry asked.

"That's the thing, nothing much. We were given make-up, clothes and told to look pretty and mingle with the guests. The one stipulation, if we spoke about what had happened to us or asked for help, we'd be killed. I got nervous but nothing bad happened, none of the men came onto us. Whoever owned the villa threw a lot of parties and appeared to simply want some eye candy around. We were told to have a good time and not to worry, that as long as we kept our mouths shut, we were safe." She put a hand up to her long hair. "At the time I reckoned it was being blonde that did it, but I was wrong. The other three girls who'd been travelling with me were also from wealthy families. They were keeping us safe while they negotiated the ransom."

"Did you try to escape?" asked Jess.

"Yes, and that's when I got this." She rolled up the sleeve of the jumper she was wearing and showed them a long thin red scar. "A man called Kamal took a knife to me. Said if I tried to run again, it would be my throat next time." She pulled a face. "That was my big mistake. I don't mean running, my mistake was getting caught. The following day I was bundled into the van again and I think that's when we left for Calais."

"Was it a long journey?" Jess asked.

"Yes. We travelled for days. Me and one other girl who I didn't know. She had no English and I had only a few words of Turkish."

"So, the others were picked up in Calais?" Jess asked.

"I believe so, from the camps. One, a girl called Mina, had paid the traffickers a fortune, believing they'd take her to a cousin in London. Most of them had been told some fairy tale to keep them sweet."

Harry shuddered. "Did you hear any other names, apart from Kamal?"

"I met his sister, Emira. From a conversation I overheard, I gleaned that the man who owned the villa was the boss of the operation in Europe. Kamal was terrified of him, I know that much."

"Do you know what these people are into?" Harry asked.

"Trafficking, drugs, anything you care to mention. It's a huge operation reaching right across the globe, and according to Kamal, obscenely profitable. The night of the party he got drunk, said too much and was more than happy to talk about the operation. I don't know much about the hierarchy but from what I put together, the top man in Europe — the one with the villa — runs many smaller groups across the continent and in the UK. Because of my attempt to escape, I was labelled 'trouble,' which was why I ended up being shipped off to the man who runs the operation in the north of England."

"The man with the villa, did you ever hear what his name was?" Harry leaned forward. If she could tell them that, it would be the major breakthrough they so badly needed.

"I only met him once. Everyone at the villa called him 'Smoke,' but he was definitely foreign. He didn't sound Turkish either, like Kamal or Emira. His accent was very different."

"What happened when you got to England?" asked Harry. He was curious to know how they'd made it through the port without any hitches. "Didn't the port authorities ask them questions?"

"No, there was no problem."

Harry made a note to pass this information onto Marcus Edge. It was probable that the gang had someone at the port on their payroll.

"Once through Dover, we drove up the motorway and parked up for ages outside Sheffield," Tracy said.

"How did you know where you were?" asked Harry. "I take it there were no windows in the back of the van?"

"No, we didn't see outside for days, but the van was old and the bodywork rusty. I scraped away at it until I made a hole I could see through." She smiled. "I did my best to remember every sign and road name."

"Clever girl," Harry said.

"Sheffield was interesting. Some men joined the ones taking us, and there was some sort of argument. Kamal wasn't happy. It sounded like things weren't ready or something. One man did most of the talking. I didn't see him, he was standing to the right of my spyhole, but I certainly heard him. He gave Kamal a right roasting, said Smoke, the boss in Europe, wouldn't be happy and that if Kamal wanted to live, he'd better put things right."

"Did Kamal use a name when he spoke to this man?"

"No, but he had a broad Scottish accent." She smiled. "A lot stronger than yours."

"Are you sure, Tracy?" Harry asked. "It was definitely Scottish, not something else?"

"I'm certain."

Harry felt his head begin to swim. That meant one thing. His instincts had been right. Salton was in charge of this operation, had to be. His old enemy was working for this Smoke, the one Tracy had met at the villa. He was one of his UK operatives, probably running the north of England.

"Does that help?" Tracy asked.

"A lot," Harry said. "You've done well."

"What'll happen to the other women and girls?" she asked. "Some of them are very young."

"Where possible they will be returned. I'm no expert but those who have no one might be able to seek asylum in the UK."

"Two of them died. The woman who escaped from the villa with me was shot by Kamal. We were running for our lives, he had a gun and shot at us. I don't think he meant to hit us, we were far more valuable alive, but he lost his temper, didn't seem to care. I was devastated when she screamed and fell but I couldn't stop, they'd have killed me too. The other one died in the van. I don't know much about these things, but I think she had appendicitis. I hammered on the van to attract the driver's attention, but he took no notice. That journey was one of the most terrifying experiences anyone can endure. I want whoever did it catching. They should spend the rest of their days locked up for what they did to us."

CHAPTER FORTY-NINE

"Tracy will be allowed to go home but we'll keep a close watch on her," Harry said. They were back in the main office.

"Poor girl," Jess said. "That was some experience. She's been brave all right, and resourceful too. And she gave us a clue, the Scottish man. That's who we need to find, Harry. Whoever he is, he's one vicious bastard."

Jess was right, but it didn't make Harry feel any better. It looked more likely than ever that the man Tracy meant was Salton, that he was behind this and was somewhere nearby. The man hated him, would kill him if he got the chance. He had to find out where he was and have him brought in urgently.

He disappeared down the stairs and made for the car park. He wanted a word with Sandy.

"I have to know where Salton is holed up," he told him. "Sandy, this is important, lives depend on me bringing him in."

"I've told you, laddie. He's living on Barra, has been on and off for six months or more."

"Is he using his own name?"

"I doubt it, but that information isn't easy to get hold of. A whisper did have him leaving last week. He may be back but I've no way of checking."

"I need to know where he is, Sandy. It's possible he was close to here recently and if he was we're in trouble. I need more information. I need to know when Salton left the island and his exact whereabouts now."

"Are you sure about this, laddie?"

"No, I'm not sure about anything but the case I'm working on has Salton stamped all over it. D'you have his Barra address, I'll have it checked out."

"Barra is tiny, you just have to ask at the shop by the jetty. You'll soon find him."

Next, Harry rang Marcus Edge and told him about Tracy and the other women.

"We are speaking to the women, and Tracy will be interviewed shortly. Regarding Salton, I'll make some enquiries and get back to you," Edge said.

"Tracy mentioned a man she met at a villa she was held at. She has no idea where this was or his real name, but the people around him called him 'Smoke.'"

"Could be useful. I'll see if anything is known about him. Given the attempt on your life, a safe house might be an idea. You are obviously considered a threat."

"I suspect that was down to Kamal. I want to bring him in," Harry said.

"Not yet. Kamal and his sister are in trouble. They've lost the merchandise and the big man won't be happy. They're more useful to us free. That way, we can be ready when they slip up."

Harry returned to the main office, where DI Maxwell was waiting for him.

"Sykes has come round. He's admitted to lying." He tossed a report onto Harry's desk. "A copy for you. You might find something in there that will help, although I can't see it. He says he found the kid wandering around on her own. When he was seen, he was taking her to the kiosk at the entrance. That's his story anyway."

"And he left her there?" Harry asked.

"So he says. With the girl who takes the money for the boat rides."

"We should have a word with her," Harry called to Jess.

"Oh, I already have. I interviewed her myself this week." Maxwell said. "She reckons the kid's mother came for her, all panicky and screaming for the child."

"Did she know who the mother was?"

"Kelsey Green." He saw the look both detectives gave him. "She did say this at the time too, but she wasn't believed — some discrepancy with the descriptions of Kelsey and the woman who took Lucy. I showed her a couple of photos of Kelsey, it was her all right."

Jess looked Harry in the eye. "Lucy didn't go missing that day at all. Kelsey faked the whole thing. I wonder what for."

"Trouble is, we can't ask her. But Lucy was still reported missing for several weeks after that and then turned up out of the blue. Why, I wonder? What happened to change things?"

"What about those traces of Lucy's blood on Sykes?" Jess asked.

"He maintains the kid had fallen and grazed her knee."

Something he'd maintained all along. "How is the CCTV examination going?" Harry asked.

"Slowly, sir," PC Carter said. "They don't have an organised system and they keep days' worth of stuff on micro discs that they don't label. Searching through them is a nightmare and it's taking all my spare time."

"Make it a priority. Colin!" He called to DC Vance. "Give him a hand."

Lucy Green had been in Shaw's Haulage yard shortly before she was found, which was the very day Sutton and Marsh went missing. Why? Find out and it could help the case.

"Your mobile's ringing." Jess nodded at his desk.

He picked it up. "You will meet me."

Harry didn't recognise the voice, but from the accent he presumed it was Kamal. "Why? We've nothing to talk about."

"You have my property. I want it back."

"Those women are no one's property, and certainly not yours."

"Was last night not warning enough? We do not play games. You have one hour to arrange something."

"And if I don't?" asked Harry.

"There will be consequences."

"Idiot!" Harry said, and threw the mobile back on his desk.

"Who was that?" Jess asked.

"One of the people who took those women. His name is Kamal and he works for whoever is behind the trafficking. I also think he was behind the fentanyl that was dished out on the Baxendale, perhaps even the killing of Sutton and Marsh too."

"The Kamal Tracy told us about? The one me and Colin saw shoving those women into that bus?" Harry nodded

"Then we should bring him in. Babs Milton too, she's bound to know things. The man is living with her."

He sighed. Jess looked so serious, so intent on getting it right. "It's not that simple. I've been told to leave him out there, him and his sister." He saw the look, the questions that would follow. "It's not just the police involved in this, Jessie. There are others. I simply do as I'm told."

CHAPTER FIFTY

"What others? What are you talking about? What's really going on?" Jess asked. "You're not involved with these people, are you?"

"Course not — not the traffickers anyway. I'm not at liberty to say more."

"That's why they tried to kill you, isn't it? Bring them in, that's my advice, before they succeed."

Jess was right, though it wouldn't please Edge. But should that still be a consideration? After all, Edge had done him no favours.

"You're making a mistake," Jess warned him. "You need to consider your career, Lennox, let alone your life. You're taking too many risks."

He smiled. "That's me all over."

"And you've nowhere to live! What are you doing about that?" Jess asked. "They've trashed the camper van and you can't live on the street. Perhaps you should get a flat, somewhere pleasant and then you can save up for a house."

He grinned. "Not my style. I prefer living at the sharp end."

"You're an idiot, d'you know that? Harry Lennox, there are times when I think I don't know you at all."

Harry gave an enigmatic little smile. Well, if this case didn't end neatly, she might find out. Collar Mungo Salton and he'd talk. But would anyone believe him? After all, it would be a villain's word against a cop's. Was it a risk he wanted to take?

Jess was staring into space. Suddenly, she flung her pen down on the desk. "We can't just leave those people out there. Kamal and his sister should be brought in, regardless of what you've been told. They're killers, the pair of them."

Jess was right to be worried. He was too, if truth be told. Kamal was violent and far too eager to please his boss. It was all very well for Marcus Edge to give out orders, but he and Jess had to live with the mayhem.

"Okay, I'll have another word with my contact," he said.

"Want to tell your partner who that is?" she asked.

"Better you don't know."

A uniformed PC put his head around the office door. "Sir, there's a body in the park. It was found draped over the roundabout, face down. Scared the kids half to death."

"Do we have an ID?"

"No, there was nothing useful on her. Her face is a bit of a mess too. Looks like she was shot in the head."

Harry saw the expression on Jess's face. This was where he got the blame for not acting sooner.

"Do we have any idea when it happened?" Harry asked, pulling his jacket off the back of the chair.

"Can't be long, the roundabout was still moving."

"We'll go and take a look. We'll ring the Reid on the way."

"Already done, sir."

* * *

"She's been dead a matter of minutes," Melanie said. "The place was empty but those kids over there heard the shot and came running."

Harry looked over to the group of young teenage boys standing with one of the uniformed officers. "They didn't see the killer, did they?"

"No, they say not, but he can't have gone far. There's a squad car out looking for him and several officers on foot."

"I'll have a word with the lads."

Harry approached the group. "Well, that must have given you a right shock."

"We heard the gun," one of them said. "Is she dead?"

"I'm afraid so," Harry said gently. "Did you approach her at all, to see what had happened?"

"Jack did," another one of them said. "But the sight of her face made him throw up. One of your lot has taken him home."

A uniformed officer hurried over to them. "A woman's spotted a man running towards the town centre, sir. Along the path over there."

"I'll take a look at the body and then take a wander." Harry went over to the body. She was face down, but he didn't need to see more. It was Emira. He knew from the long, lustrous black hair. She'd been right about Kamal. Brother or not, he'd killed her, and it was his, Harry's, fault. She wanted out. She'd asked him for help, and he'd ignored her.

He walked over to the officer with the group of lads. "Make sure they get home," he said, "and that they're not left alone. Have a word with the parents."

Jess came marching towards him, furious. "He's on the rampage, with a gun. He should have been in custody, now she's dead. Who'll be next, Harry? You need to decide where your loyalties lie, because this is getting out of hand. Who does this Kamal work with and what's his problem?"

Harry had to give her something. "The trafficked women — he wants them back. His own life depends on it. The dead woman is his sister, Emira. That's a measure of how desperate he is. Whoever is controlling Kamal will not like how this has turned out."

"We shouldn't have let this happen. You knew about him, and he's been named often enough in this case."

Harry knew she was right. But why kill Emira? Did he plan to run? Was Kamal getting rid of the evidence, making sure there was no one left to point the finger? But if that was so, what about him? He knew more than anyone what Kamal had done and who was behind it all.

"Give me a minute," he told Jess. Harry moved out of earshot and rang Marcus Edge. "Emira is dead," he said angrily. "Shot by her brother. This is where our agreement ends. I've had enough. I need the freedom to do my job properly and working with you doesn't give me that." He cut the call and went back to join Jess.

"I need to ensure that Martha and her clan are safe. I'll get them some protection."

"You're with me on this now, are you? We bring this lunatic in?"

"Yes, Jessie, we do."

CHAPTER FIFTY-ONE

"I'm bleary eyed with it," PC Carter complained. "I'll see this stretch of road in my sleep. I know practically every inch of the roads around Stamford Park."

"Anything helpful?" Colin Vance asked.

"I don't know what I'm looking for. I haven't seen anyone I recognise. But on the plus side, I have found the film from the morning in question, all four hours of it. So, if the DI cares to take a look, he might spot something himself."

"You can leave it with me now if you like, I'll pass it on," Vance said.

"I know what this is," PC Carter said. "I do the work and you take all the glory. You want on his team, don't you? You always were an ambitious sod. I remember you at school, right little teacher's pet, you were."

"So, I'm ambitious. Where's the harm in that? I like working with DI Lennox and Jess, and there's only two of them which means their team is light on bodies."

"Okay, I give in. I just hope it does you some good." PC Carter stomped out of the office.

Colin Vance sat down at the computer and took a look for himself. Carter hadn't been joking when he said there was nothing much to see, just a stream of cars. It was possible to make out who was driving some of them but not all. Hopefully, something would catch the DI's eye.

Carter was right. Colin was keen to make a name for himself and he saw working with Lennox as a definite plus. He was younger than DI Maxwell and had a good clear up record. It would do his career prospects no harm to be one of Lennox's team.

Angela called across the office. "Where is everyone?"

"There's been a murder in the park. A woman. Something to do with the trafficking case."

"Poor thing," she said. "Oh, and word of advice. You might have to suggest joining Harry's team yourself. He's a bit slow on the uptake at times."

"How do I do that? He might think I'm being pushy."

"You have to be pushy, Colin, if you want to get on. Harry appreciates ambition, he'll think all the more of you for it."

Colin phoned Harry to tell him about the CCTV footage. "We've got it down to four hours, sir. There's not a lot of traffic, it was early, but I don't recognise anyone. It struck me that you might, you being more involved with the case."

"Good work, Colin. I'll come in soon and take a look."

* * *

"Colin's whittled down the CCTV from the park to something I can look at," Harry told Jess.

"Can't that wait? We've got Kamal to find, and now Hettie wants you." She pointed to the figure waving at them from a distance.

"Kamal could be anywhere. Uniform will check Babs Milton's place and Martha's, plus anywhere else that's been connected with the case. There's not much we can do."

Harry went to have a word with Hettie and Melanie.

"One shot to the back of the head, exiting via the face," Melanie said with a grimace. "She didn't suffer, it'd have been quick. The same shotgun as killed the others, I reckon. I picked this up off the grass." It was a spent cartridge.

"Check it, will you?" Emira was dead and he, Harry, was to blame. He hadn't taken her seriously. But if she was that afraid, why not contact him?

"Are we going for that walk round town or what?" Jess asked.

"I don't see the point. He's alone, armed and desperate to get those women back. He is one dangerous man and we do nothing without backup. There's a team on it, we'd just be superfluous."

The phone Emira had given him buzzed in his pocket. Unknown number. Kamal! Had to be.

"You should hand yourself in," Harry said.

"You will do as I tell you. Refuse and more people will die, starting with that woman I have been living with."

"Babs? Why would you hurt her? She's helped you, looked after the factory."

"I have just killed my own sister. Babs is nothing to me. I have her here. She will die, I promise you. Meet me and we will talk. Then you will do as you are told."

"Just let me think a second." He covered the handset. "Is anyone with Babs? Is she safe?" Harry mouthed at Jess. He watched her get her mobile and make a brief call. She shook her head.

"Okay," Harry said to Kamal. "Where?"

"The factory. And come alone." He ended the call.

"Kamal wants to meet me at the factory. He's holding Babs and he's threatening to kill her if I don't agree."

"You cannot walk into this on your own, Lennox. No way. You will organise backup or I'll do it for you."

"The merest whiff of police and who knows what he'll do."

"Rubbish, you're not invincible. A bullet will kill you as easily as anyone else."

"Okay, we'll get back to the office and sort it."

CHAPTER FIFTY-TWO

Within the hour, armed response had been mobilised, and Harry was preparing for the meeting with Kamal.

"I hate these things," he said, fiddling with the bullet-proof vest he was wearing.

"You've no choice," Jess said.

"We get a clear shot, we'll take him out," the armed response commander told Harry.

"I'd prefer him alive, and I think the NCA would too."

"What have they got to do with this?" Jess asked. Why had Harry said nothing to her, and why had he been singled out?

"I've been working with a Marcus Edge, one of their investigators." He looked at the armed response commander. "You might contact him, let him know what's about to happen."

"Any more secrets I should know about?" Jess asked.

"Yes, but they aren't for sharing, not yet."

* * *

They were about ready to leave for the factory when the office phone rang. It was Gregor Laing for Jess. "I have to take this," she said. "I'll catch you up."

The others left and Jess sat down ready to make notes. What Laing had to say could be important, sort Harry's head.

"I have some news for you. Might not be what you want to hear, but here goes," he began. "We were given information about an impending drug deal. A large amount of heroin was to change hands at a location up in the hills above Glasgow. We intercepted, some of the dealers were arrested and during the interviews we were given information about two murders. We checked the alleged burial site and right enough we found the bodies. One of them is Callum McBain, there's no doubt about it. This man is known to Harry and I know he has been asking about him. Reassure Harry that we did DNA, dental records, the lot. There is no mistake. McBain is dead. There is no doubt he was murdered. Information received puts this down to him crossing a man called Fernal Mehmed. He wanted to recruit McBain, but the villain refused."

That made sense. They knew Mehmed and what had happened to Sutton and Marsh. Jess was also aware that the man in charge was Scottish, so it made sense that known villains were preferred for the Ryebridge operation.

"What about Salton? Anything on him?" Jess asked. "We believe he's behind what is happening on our patch."

"Quite possibly. He is still alive and active, I'm afraid. The man has been holed up on the Isle of Barra these last months, orchestrating something no doubt. I know Harry was hoping he was dead, but that's not the case. We have recent evidence to the contrary."

"Thanks for the information. Do you know what Salton has on Harry?"

"No, and I'd let it drop if I was you. Harry Lennox deserves some peace."

Jess opened her mouth to ask more but Laing had gone.

* * *

From outside, the factory looked closed. Harry pulled into the car park and waited. Looking up, he could see the armed officers making their way across the roof.

His mobile rang, it was the armed response commander.

"We're in position. Word of warning, don't go inside. Wait for him to come out to you. We want a clean shot."

Good call, but would it solve anything? With Kamal dead, they'd get no answers, no one to point the finger at Salton. His mobile rang again. This time it was Jess.

"Good luck, idiot, and remember, don't take any risks."

He heard the fear in her voice. Jess was worried for his safety.

"I have news, whether you like it or not you need to know," she said. "I've had Gregor Laing on from Glasgow. Mungo Salton is very much alive. Your instincts could be right, it's possible Salton is the man behind this operation. McBain is dead, he has been for a few months. They've found the grave, done tests, the lot. It's definitely him, so whatever it is between the two of you, he's no longer a problem."

Salton still alive? On the personal front, not good news. But where the case was concerned, it fitted with his theory. Harry had him earmarked as the head man in the north of England. Who else could it be but Salton?

Harry's head was all over the place as he tried to work it out. He'd been sure all along, and Sandy had backed him up. What he had to do now was get the evidence to nail the bastard, put him away for life for what he'd done. If only the prospect of jousting with his old enemy didn't fill him with so much dread. He stared at the factory windows — someone was watching him through a chink in the blinds. Kamal? Had to be. Sod armed response, this was getting them nowhere. He got out of the car and took a few steps forwards.

Babs appeared at the main door. She looked terrified.

"He's lost it," she screamed at him. "He's cut my arm. He wants to kill me."

He could see the blood dripping onto the ground. Babs Milton needed help.

"Kamal!" he shouted. "Come out and we'll talk."

"He wants you in here," Babs shouted back. "If you don't come in, he'll hurt me more."

214

Harry didn't want that. She might have helped Kamal in the past, but Babs had had no idea what she was dealing with.

Up on the roof, one of the armed response officers was waving frantically, indicating for him to back off. But leave Kamal to appear and Babs would be dead. Harry couldn't live with another dead woman on his conscience.

"I'm coming in!" he shouted so everyone could hear. "Tell Kamal I want to cut a deal."

CHAPTER FIFTY-THREE

"What're you up to?" Jess asked Colin Vance. "You've had your face glued to that screen for hours."

"It's the CCTV. I've got the right period of time but it's all meaningless to me. I did spot an SUV, but I didn't recognise the driver. Probably just someone passing by."

"Let me have a look," Jess said.

She spent a few minutes painstakingly going through each frame of video. "There. That's a likely contender. The tyre tracks we took could have come from something similar." She tried to enlarge the image of the driver but could only get the back of his head. "He's got grey hair," she announced. "Is there any chance we could pick this vehicle up further down the road? We might get his face then."

"I've got the film from the next camera along. Let me try." Colin Vance sat down and stopped the film as the SUV got within range of the camera. "Got him. Look, it's pretty clear, but I still don't know him."

Jess did though. She stared at the image, wondering what it meant, how it was possible. She needed an urgent word with Harry. He had to know about this at once.

* * *

"You are a fool," Kamal sneered. "They would have given you money, made you rich."

"Well, money isn't everything. I like my job, thanks, and I fancy hanging onto it."

"You are going to die," Kamal said.

"Yeah, yeah. I've heard it all before. Tougher men than you have tried to kill me, Kamal, and I'm still here."

"Ah yes, I heard something about that. A fire, wasn't it? Like the other night. Shame you were out."

"I was with your sister." Harry was deliberately taunting him now. "She liked me. She told me all about you and how badly you treated her."

"She was using you."

"So why kill her then?"

"Trisha was too independent, liked to do things her way. The boss doesn't like that in anyone. I was told to kill her."

"Orders, eh. Shame that, and her being your sister too. Do everything the boss says, do you? Not got a mind of your own? That's a pity, because if you could think for yourself, you'd see that there's no way out of this for you." Harry went to the window and pulled up the blind. "Have you looked outside, Kamal? Spotted the troops yet?"

Babs screamed. Kamal had a knife at her throat.

"Let her go," Harry said, "She has done nothing to hurt you or your operation."

Suddenly, Babs kicked out backwards. Her high-heel caught Kamal on the shin and he cried out in pain. Grabbing her chance she knocked his arm hard and he dropped the knife.

"Run!" Harry ordered her. "Get out now."

She didn't hesitate. Now the two men were alone, facing each other. "Want to live, Kamal?"

Kamal had dropped the knife, but he still held the shotgun. He gave Harry a look of pure hate. "Do you? My orders are to kill you."

"Orders from who? Does he have a name, this mysterious boss of yours who tells you what to do? He even goes as far as ordering you to kill your own sister, no less." Harry tutted. "It's a poor show that, Kamal. I couldn't do it."

"I do it because I want to live," Kamal said. "And he pays me well."

"A name, Kamal, and then we're done. The men out there will take you in and offer you protection. You'll be safe. Your boss, whoever he is, won't be able to touch you."

"You are a fool if you believe that."

Harry's mobile vibrated in his pocket. "Time's up," he said. "Sorry we didn't reach an agreement. Well, it's your loss. You should have taken what was offered."

Despite his brave words, Harry was terrified. This had to end well, it had to, he didn't want a bullet in his head and this man was desperate. He began to inch backwards, slowly, in the direction of the door. Would Kamal fire that gun? It didn't take long to find out. Harry was only inches from the door when a bullet whistled past his left ear and buried itself in the wall.

"Next time it will be your head."

"You don't really want this, Kamal. Just let me go, give yourself up and we can work it out."

Kamal raised the gun. "No more talk. I am finished with you."

Harry closed his eyes. This was it. Kamal couldn't miss this time. Then a shot rang out and Kamal fell to the ground. Harry stumbled backwards and steadied himself against the wall, watching blankly as the armed response team poured into the shed.

CHAPTER FIFTY-FOUR

The yard outside the factory was suddenly full of people. Harry was taken to a waiting ambulance and checked over.

"Apart from shattered nerves, I'm fine," he said to the paramedic. He held out his hand. "Look, I'm still shaking."

She smiled at him. "You're a brave lad, from what I hear."

Harry suddenly noticed how pretty the paramedic was. "Goes with the job," he said, giving her one of his charming smiles. "Oh, what about Babs. Is she okay?"

"She's gone to the hospital, but the cut is superficial, she'll be fine."

"That's good. Makes it all worthwhile."

"Well, I think you deserve a medal, taking on a gunman like that and saving a woman's life."

"He's a regular knight in shining armour is our Harry." Jess climbed into the ambulance. "You were told not to go in there. So, what happened?"

"He would have killed Babs," Harry said. "I didn't want another life lost, so I did what I had to. Problem is, Kamal took the name of the big boss with him. I'm no closer to knowing who is running the north of England operation than I ever was."

Jess sat down next to him. "I might be able to help you there." She smiled. "D'you need this?" She tugged on the blanket the paramedic had wrapped around his shoulders. "Only, we should get going."

"No, I don't. What I really need is a strong whiskey. Hang on. What did you mean? How can you help?"

"I know who he is," she said, and smiled at him.

Harry stared at her, uncomprehending. How was this even possible? Jess didn't know the case like he did.

"You've got proof?"

"That might be tricky, we have to piece everything together first. We need to speak to Tracy again, she might be able to help, and forensics of course."

"His name, Jess. Put me out of my misery."

"Not Salton, despite your instincts. My money is on Sandy Munroe."

Harry stared at her. This must be some kind of joke. Well, he didn't see the humour. No way was any of it down to Sandy. It couldn't be, he'd known that man most of his life. "What's given you that wild idea?"

"He'd already been in Ryebridge several days before he went to see you."

"How d'you know that?"

"Because it was him who dropped Lucy Green off at the park that morning. We've got him on CCTV — date and time stamped, the lot."

Harry tried to think this through, but his head was too full of what had just happened. "Not Sandy. You must have it wrong. This little lot is all down to Salton."

"Come back to the office and see for yourself," she said. "It's definitely him on the CCTV. I was as surprised as you, Harry. But if you weigh it all up, it makes sense. Tracy heard a Scottish accent, naturally you presumed it was Salton speaking but it had to have been Sandy."

"Look there are loads of villains with Scottish accents — believe me, I've caught enough of them."

"He's your old boss, I get it. You don't want to believe he's capable of this. But you must consider it, given the evidence."

"I'll speak to him," Harry said.

"Probably not a good idea. You are compromised, him being a friend and all that."

"He isn't, not anymore," Harry said. "If you're right and this is down to Sandy, I'll never forgive him."

"Let's go back to the station — if you're up to it that is — and we'll go from there. If you do call him, we can trace it. That will tell us where he is," Jess said.

"Well, he's in Glasgow. He went home, remember?"

"We'll see. Right now, I want to know how he got Lucy Green into his car, and what she was doing in that yard."

"She had to have been with someone, Jess, that means Summer or Marsh. But what did either of them have to do with the child's disappearance?"

"I've been thinking about that. I reckon we should have another chat with Caroline. Remember her saying something about wanting kids? What if she struck a deal with Kelsey, paid her for Lucy?"

Surely not. That was an awful idea. What mother would sell their child? "You think Kelsey could really do that?"

"For money, yes, I do, Jessie. It would enable her to buy all the drugs and booze she needed."

"But she didn't have money. We found no cash in her flat."

"If my theory is right, Kelsey would have given it to her dealer within hours of receiving it. She's not the saving type and I doubt there's a bank account, but I've got Colin checking that one. We need that word with Caroline," Harry said.

"Want to go now? Are you up to it?" she asked.

"Yeah, I'll be fine."

"I'd better drive. You're still shaking."

CHAPTER FIFTY-FIVE

Caroline Sutton looked stunned. "You think I stole that child?"

"No, but we think you colluded with Kelsey to let you take her on as your own. In fact, the entire time Lucy was supposedly missing, she was here with you."

Caroline looked outraged. "You're mad, the pair of you. How would I get away with that? The whole town was looking for her. Her photo was in all the papers."

"You kept her hidden," Harry said. "A house and garden this large and secluded, it wouldn't be difficult."

"People come here, Joan works here and what about Nick? How would I hide her from him?"

"D'you keep chickens?" Jess asked.

"Yes. Why do you ask?"

"You see, forensic tests on the soles of Lucy's shoes have found chicken feed on them. And there's the puzzle of Clara. At first, I thought she was talking about a toy, but she wasn't, was she, Caroline? Lucy was talking about a real chicken."

Caroline stared at Jess for a few moments. Then she seemed to deflate. "She loved that chicken," she said through her tears. "Clara hatched out while Lucy was here. The child was captivated, she wanted to keep her."

"What happened, Caroline?" Harry asked. "How did Lucy end up in the haulage yard where we found your husband's body?"

"I'm not sure, but that morning Nick said he'd had enough. He knew what I'd done, about the arrangement with Kelsey, but he didn't like any of it. He kept quiet for a few weeks but it was never going to last. He said she had to go back to her mother. I tried talking to him. I begged him, but he wouldn't listen. When he left the house, he bundled her into his car with the intention of taking her back. He obviously didn't get there. I can only presume that at some point during that journey he was taken, along with Lucy."

That made sense. But whoever took him had set the child free. Knowing Kamal like he did, Harry knew that wasn't his style. He showed no mercy, not even to his sister, so why let a strange child go?

"Did you pay Kelsey?" Jess asked.

"Yes, we had an arrangement. I paid her a regular amount in cash each week. Joan used to see to that for me. She was in on the secret too. She found it hard, knew it was wrong but she also knew Kelsey and the life Lucy would have if the child stayed with her."

"Thank you for being honest with us," Harry said. "It might help us catch the men who killed Nick."

"Those shoes, the mistake you made was allowing Kelsey to pick them up after Lucy disappeared. Why not just have them delivered?" Jess asked.

"Because we're local and we have no children. I was terrified that Allen's might have asked questions, told people. I was desperate not to be found out. I wanted to keep Lucy safe, love her as my own."

* * *

"What do we do about her?" Jess asked as they went back to the car.

"There was no actual kidnap. It could be argued that all Caroline was doing was a spot of child minding for Kelsey. She had Kelsey's permission, after all."

"That's a bit far-fetched. Kelsey sold her daughter and Social Services need to be told."

Harry didn't see the point. "Told what? What would they do? Kelsey is dead, and Lucy is safe. I don't see where prosecuting Caroline would get anyone. Hasn't that woman suffered enough?"

"That's not our call to make, Harry."

"I'm more concerned about sorting the case. Finding Sandy for a start — if that's really who's at the bottom of it all."

"He is," Jess said confidently.

Harry rang the Reid. "Hettie, we're after more evidence to build a case. The pathway where the child's shoes were found, did your people get anything else?"

"We did a sweep but got nothing. The street cleaners had been in two days previous, so there's nothing to find."

"Ah well. It was a long shot anyway."

He turned to Jess. "On the way in, we'll stop off at the Bluebell, the B&B I've been staying at. I went there because Sandy recommended it. We can check the date of his arrival."

Harry was certain there had to be some mistake and confirming the exact dates of Sandy's stay would help. But they were in for a surprise. Apparently, Sandy hadn't stayed there at all. A check on the register showed there had been no new visitors around the dates in question, and definitely no one of that name.

"He lied," Jess said. "Why would he do that if he was on the level?"

"I still don't understand but I agree. Let's get to the office and I'll ring him. I hope we're wrong, Jessie, this is all I need."

CHAPTER FIFTY-SIX

"Are you all right, sir? I heard about what happened," Colin Vance said when Harry and Jess walked in

"I'm fine. Regular hero me. Man with shotgun, bring it on," Harry said.

"Take no notice, Colin, he's an idiot. He could have got himself killed back there."

Harry gave Jess a disapproving look. "That's no way to talk about me to the newest member of the team. He's supposed to look up to me, even be slightly in awe."

Harry winked at Colin, who was almost jumping up and down in his excitement. "D'you mean it, sir? Am I really in?"

"Subject to Rodders's approval, but I don't see any problem. We need another person on the team."

"I checked if Kelsey Green had a bank account like you asked," Colin said. "She didn't."

"As I expected, poor cow, that's no way to live. The cash she got off Caroline was drugs money, and that's all she needed," Jess shuddered. "Lucy was well out of it."

Harry had Sandy's mobile number up on his screen ready to call him. "Get the tech guys to trace the call I'm about to make," he told Vance. "I want to know the whereabouts of the man I'm ringing. He may still be in the area, but I want to make sure."

Colin was on the office phone immediately, setting it up. Harry was waiting for the off when Rodders walked in.

"Harry. My office."

"Have them hold that until I return," Harry said.

"I wonder what that's all about," Colin said.

"Who knows?" Jess said. "Well, back to the paperwork for us."

A uniformed officer stuck his head around the door. "DS Wilde, there's a woman in reception asking for you."

"I'd better go down," she said.

The woman turned out to be Anthea, Harry's ex. "I hope you don't mind. I asked for Harry but he's in a meeting apparently. I wanted to leave this for him." She handed Jess a shoe box. "He came for his stuff. Most of it was in the shed but I'd kept this in the house for safe keeping. It's his grandfather's medals and two gold watches."

"Thanks, Anthea, I'll make sure he gets them." Jess wondered if this was the right time to ask. Well, why not? "Actually, I've been meaning to speak to you about Harry. When you were together, did he ever talk about his past, his life on the force in Glasgow?"

Anthea pulled a face. "It was his past that tore us apart." She sighed and turned to stare out of the window. "I liked Harry, I really did, but I couldn't put up with the way he was any longer. He's tormented, Jess. His past won't let him go. The nightmares, the screaming, it all became too much. I asked him over and over to just talk to me, but he always refused. In the end, I finished it. It was the easiest way out for both of us."

"He didn't mention his family or people he used to work with — Sandy or Morag for instance?"

"A brief mention of Morag, a card at Christmas, but nothing much. Where Harry's concerned, the present is all that matters. It's as if the past did not exist."

* * *

Harry entered Rodders's office to find a visitor — Marcus Edge. He turned to the super. "What's he doing here?"

"Your team has worked hard on the case, and brought it to a satisfactory close," Edge told him. "But now it's time to hand over to us."

Harry looked at Rodders. "You can't sanction this! We're within a spit of catching the villain that killed Marsh and Sutton."

"Yes, I know, and so does he, which is why Sandy Munroe has handed himself in."

Harry stared blankly at Edge, barely able to believe what he'd just heard. He had been hoping that Jess's theory was wrong, and Sandy had nothing to do with the case. Some hope.

"He's done a deal, I suppose. What have you offered him?" Harry asked.

"He'll do time, no fear of him getting out of that," Rodders confirmed. "But a short sentence, after which he'll disappear, never to be heard of again. New identity, new place to live, you know the drill."

Indeed, he did. But it wasn't good enough in Harry's eyes. Why let him off so lightly? "He killed two men — or arranged for it to happen. He created mayhem in this town. The fentanyl — have you forgotten that? He had to be the one issuing the orders which Kamal followed, resulting in three deaths apart from Sutton and Marsh. And we're helping him to walk? It does my head in."

"We have no choice, Harry," Edge said. "Munroe is going to give me everything we need to crack the European side of the operation — names and all — including the whereabouts of the man known as 'Smoke.'"

But Harry wasn't satisfied. "Can't you get Europol on the case or something? Do it the correct way?"

"We don't have the time. Smoke will go into hiding and we'll miss our chance. This is how it is to be." Edge sounded impatient. "Accept it, take the praise and move on."

Harry knew he had no choice. This was probably what Edge had had in mind all along. CID would do the groundwork, catch the killer, and then he'd step in and clean up. "Has Sandy said anything?"

"What about?" Rodders asked.

"Me."

The super shook his head, but Edge cleared his throat and looked away. Harry caught the look. So, he had said something.

"But he has asked to see you, you and your partner Jess," Rodders said.

"He wants to apologise is what he said," Edge added. "He feels bad about how things have turned out."

Harry nodded. "Now okay for you?"

"We have him at a secure location. I'll drive you," Edge said. "I'll meet you and your DS outside in ten minutes."

Harry wasn't happy with any of it, but what could he do? Nothing. Well, at least he'd get to tell the bastard what he thought of him.

Back in the office, he told Colin to forget the trace. "It's not happening now. Jess, we're going out."

"There was me all psyched up to make the big arrest," she said.

"Not our call this time. That's been taken care of, it's out of our hands. Come on, this is important."

Jess took one look at his face and grabbed her coat.

EPILOGUE

The accommodation they'd put Sandy in was a lot more comfortable than a prison cell. The armed guards on the door were small consolation.

"Protection," Sandy explained, "rather than stopping me from escaping. Those I work for won't want me spilling my guts to the NCA, but what the hell? They've given me a way out."

Harry could hardly contain his rage. Being told about Sandy's crime was one thing, but seeing him, knowing it was true, made his blood boil. "How the hell did you get into this in the first place? You had a good career. You had Morag, a life back home. I don't understand why you'd risk all that."

Harry was seething, he simply didn't understand the man or his motives.

"Like you, laddie. I crossed Salton." He smiled. "But unlike you, I chose a different way to deal with the fallout. I didn't run away and hide, I changed my mind, took the money, did as he asked and for a while gave the man the information he wanted. But there is always someone bigger and uglier waiting in the wings. And tough as he is, Salton won't last for ever. I was offered a job by a group operating in Europe, and a deal I couldn't refuse."

"The people traffickers. You're a right piece of work, Sandy. This isn't you. You were never that bent."

"He can't be all bad," Jess interceded. "Lucy, the little girl, it was you that saved her, wasn't it?"

"Yes. I found the wee lass cowering in the back of Sutton's car. If Kamal had seen her — well, you know what he'd have done. I'm a lot of things but not a child killer, Jess. I took her to the park and let her go."

He turned back to Harry.

"I don't want us to argue, laddie. I'd really like us to part comfortable with each other."

"Sandy, I can't do that." Harry was exasperated. "You killed people. Lucy aside, you are as bad as Salton and the rest. You pretended to be my friend, but you used me. You said you came to Ryebridge to visit me, but you were here to set things up, weren't you? You brought the entire scam to my patch. What did you expect? That I'd fall in with your plans, give you a hand? You aren't Sandy Munroe anymore. In fact, I don't know who the hell you are."

"And what about you, laddie? Who are you pretending to be?" Sandy spat this out, his eyes red and accusing.

Harry stared at him while the seconds ticked by. "Leave us, Jessie," he said at last.

"No, lass, stay. You should hear this," Sandy insisted, his eyes never leaving Harry's.

"Harry? What's he talking about?" Jess said.

Harry made an angry gesture. "It's a load of nonsense. Take no notice."

"He used to have a brother. Did you know that?" Sandy said.

Jess nodded.

"Bet you didn't know they were twins, identical twins at that. No one could tell them apart when they were growing up. Even their own parents had problems." Sandy looked at Harry. "The number of times you two swapped places. Bet you can't count them, can you, particularly when you were teens."

"Where's this going?" Jess asked, looking from one to the other of them.

"Nowhere," Harry said flatly.

"Harry Lennox was a CID officer on the trail of a villain called Mungo Salton. Salton was a cruel bastard. He wanted Harry in his pocket and when he refused, the villain threatened Harry's family, set fire to their home. Their dad was killed. Dreadful business, nothing anyone could do. The place went up in seconds, a regular inferno it was."

"That's enough now, Sandy. Stop," Harry said.

"Both young men went into that house to try to rescue their dad — Harry the detective and his twin brother, Paul. By this time the place was well alight and there was no way their father could still be alive. Nevertheless, they tried. Eventually, one twin staggered out, dragging the other by the arms. The one who made it had his hands badly burned. He also had the CID warrant badge for Harry Lennox tucked into his shirt pocket. The other one died."

Jess didn't understand. It was a tragic story and explained a lot about Harry, but why hide it from everyone? Grief? "So, Harry made it. It was terrible about his dad and his brother, but why make such a thing of it? Harry didn't start the fire."

"No, he didn't," Sandy said. "Salton did. But the incident puzzled me. A warrant badge is one thing, but Harry's work mobile was found on Paul's body, we never got to the bottom of that one. And there was another thing, the twin who died had a scar on the back of his head. As a lad, Harry had cut his head badly when he fell out of a tree onto a pile of bricks. I know because it was me that took him to get it stitched. Nothing like that had happened to Paul."

Jess glanced at Harry. "Well?"

"Well nothing. He's lying through his teeth. Perhaps he's trying to ruin my credibility. If you doubt my identity, Jess, check the police database. You'll find DNA belonging to DI Harry Lennox. I'll happily give you a fresh sample for comparison."

Sandy Munroe laughed. "Proves nothing, lass. Think about it."

Jess wasn't sure what he meant, but she was too tired to work it out. "He's lying, isn't he?"

"Yes," said Harry. "He's having one last try at ruining my career. Well, it won't work. We're leaving."

At the door he turned and took one last look at Sandy. "What a pity it had to end like this. I was really fond of you, you know. When I lost my dad, you took his place for a while. Good luck."

Harry needed air and he was shaking again. He smiled at Jess. "Now you know."

"The cut-down version is he thinks you're your twin brother, Paul, and not a detective in CID."

Harry took her arm and led her towards the waiting car. He shook his head ruefully. "A crazy idea. As if I could get away with that one."

THE END

FREE KINDLE BOOKS

Please join our mailing list for free Kindle books
and new releases, including crime thrillers, mysteries,
romance and more.

www.joffebooks.com

Follow us on Facebook, Twitter and Instagram
@joffebooks

DO YOU LOVE FREE AND BARGAIN BOOKS?

Thank you for reading this book. If you enjoyed it
please leave feedback on Amazon or Goodreads, and if
there is anything we missed or you have a question about
then please get in touch. The author and publishing team
appreciate your feedback and time reading this book.

We hate typos too but sometimes they slip through.
Please send any errors you find to
corrections@joffebooks.com.
We'll get them fixed ASAP. We're very grateful
to eagle-eyed readers who take the time to contact us.

Made in the USA
Monee, IL
29 October 2020

46310173R00142